She was ri... existing, not ... fighting off ... get close to him.

Including Jess. His beautiful Jess.

Damn it, he'd acted like a fool, distancing himself from the most precious person in his life.

He loved her. The thought slammed into him hard.

How had he been so blind to what he'd had? Was it too late to reverse the damage? It had better not be. It was time to stop running.

It was time to start loving.

Always an avid reader, **Fiona Lowe** decided to combine her love of romance with her interest in all things medical, so writing Medical Romance™ was an obvious choice! She lives in a seaside town in southern Australia, where she juggles writing, reading, working and raising two gorgeous sons with the support of her own real-life hero! You can visit Fiona's website at www.fionalowe.com

Recent titles by the same author:

PREGNANT ON ARRIVAL

THE NURSE'S LONGED-FOR FAMILY

BY
FIONA LOWE

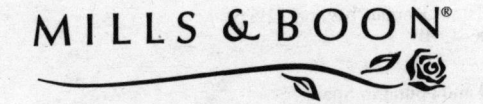

MILLS & BOON

DID YOU PURCHASE THIS BOOK WITHOUT A COVER?

If you did, you should be aware it is **stolen property** as it was reported *unsold and destroyed* by a retailer. Neither the author nor the publisher has received any payment for this book.

All the characters in this book have no existence outside the imagination of the author, and have no relation whatsoever to anyone bearing the same name or names. They are not even distantly inspired by any individual known or unknown to the author, and all the incidents are pure invention.

All Rights Reserved including the right of reproduction in whole or in part in any form. This edition is published by arrangement with Harlequin Enterprises II B.V. The text of this publication or any part thereof may not be reproduced or transmitted in any form or by any means, electronic or mechanical, including photocopying, recording, storage in an information retrieval system, or otherwise, without the written permission of the publisher.

This book is sold subject to the condition that it shall not, by way of trade or otherwise, be lent, resold, hired out or otherwise circulated without the prior consent of the publisher in any form of binding or cover other than that in which it is published and without a similar condition including this condition being imposed on the subsequent purchaser.

MILLS & BOON and MILLS & BOON with the Rose Device are registered trademarks of the publisher.

First published in Great Britain 2006
Harlequin Mills & Boon Limited,
Eton House, 18-24 Paradise Road, Richmond, Surrey TW9 1SR

© Fiona Lowe 2006

ISBN-13: 978 0 263 84756 7
ISBN-10: 0 263 84756 X

Set in Times Roman 10½ on 12½ pt
03-0906-43901

Printed and bound in Spain
by Litografia Rosés, S.A., Barcelona

THE NURSE'S LONGED-FOR FAMILY

To the wonderful heroes in my life: Norm, Sandon and Barton. Thank you for your love, your support and your faith that this work would one day be a book.

CHAPTER ONE

JESS HENDERSON gave a final wave as Dr David Parkinson's four-wheel-drive turned the corner. A selfish sadness tightened in a circle around her heart as the vehicle and the great family inside it disappeared from view.

She faced three months without the warm and loving presence of the family she'd come to love. David and his wife had given her a job as their practice nurse at the Community Health Centre when her sister's death had forced her to come to Roseport two short months ago. But, more than a job, they'd welcomed her, and helped her adjust to her new role as mother to her small nephew Woody.

She sighed. Three months without their support.

Three months working with a doctor she'd only met half an hour ago. A doctor who didn't look comfortable in his new surroundings. In fact, he didn't look happy at all.

He looked to be a totally different personality from David. But first impressions could be wrong. During their brief introductions she'd got the gut feeling he didn't really want to be in Roseport.

But, the sooner she got to know him, the better she would feel. And if that involved making polite conversation, then so be it.

She took a quick sideways glance at Dr Alexander Fitzwilliam. The man David called Alex. He looked out of place in the seaside town wearing an impeccable designer suit. At six foot one, he towered over her. Usually her five foot four inches felt tall enough, but not today. His presence seemed to dwarf her, and she was *very* aware of him.

His dark tailored suit accentuated his broad shoulders, and the jacket fell open to reveal a flat, taut stomach. Pleated trousers clung to narrow hips, emphasising his long legs. The soft material teasingly hinted at what lay underneath.

Jess fleetingly wondered what he would look like in Roseport's signature dress code of shorts. Or in a wetsuit, slick with water. Her breath caught in her throat.

She risked a quick glance upward, tilting her chin to see his face. His red hair, streaked with blond tips, seemed to be more in keeping with Roseport's relaxed lifestyle. It hit his collar, giving him a boyish look at odds with his citified air. His clear turquoise-green eyes matched the colour of the water of Roseport Bay, and right now they were staring straight at her.

A flush of heat travelled through her, surprising her. She squashed it immediately. She had no time in her life for an attraction to a locum doctor. Besides, she was flat out learning how to be a mother to twenty-two-month-old Woody.

'So, they've gone and we're here.' He looked down at Jess and gave her a tight half-smile.

'Yes, Doctor, so it seems.' Arrgh—how tongue-tied and inane could she possibly sound? But something about Dr Fitzwilliam made her feel gauche.

'Call me Alex. Everyone does—except my mother, when I've upset her, and then I get Alexander.' He grinned at the thought. The tension so evident on his face since arriving this morning slid away, and a dimple appeared in his cheek.

Jess's breath caught again. When he relaxed he was drop-dead gorgeous. *Get a grip, girl.* 'Right, Alex it is. Unless, of course, you leave the treatment room like a pigsty. Then I might join your mum in calling you Alexander.'

He laughed. 'I'll bear that in mind.' He put his hands in his pockets. 'So I guess you should show me the ropes—where things are kept, stuff like that. David did dump this on me at extremely short notice, so I'm glad you've been here a while.'

'Actually, I've only been in Roseport a couple of months myself.'

Surprise crossed his face. 'Typical David. Always dashing off to far-flung Third World places at a moment's notice, assuming the people at home will man the fort. Well, I guess we'll muddle through together.' This time his smile was a full smile, involving his eyes, which darkened slightly to sea-emerald-green.

His smile did the strangest thing to her. It was like warm sunlight beaming into the dark corners of her soul. A place that had been bereft of light recently, since her sister's death.

And Robert's betrayal.

Jess, I don't want an instant family, and I'm not fathering someone else's kid.

Jess squashed Robert's chilling voice and concentrated on talking to Alex. She gave in to her curiosity. Besides, this was part of the getting-to-know-you process. 'So you and David know each other pretty well?'

He nodded. 'We met at med school as idealistic wannabe doctors. David has a habit of pulling everyone along with his plans.' Warmth infused his words.

Jess laughed and relaxed. Her first impression of a reserved and uptight doctor was fading. Along with her apprehension about working with him. 'I know what you mean. His enthusiasm is infectious. So you've been friends ever since?'

'We have. After our intern year we travelled the world together.'

'Backpacking?' Jess fondly recalled her own adventures in Europe.

'We did a bit of that, but mostly David had us working in remote villages. We worked hard and played hard. I guess we grew into men together.'

Alex's suit spoke of a city practice at odds with what he'd just described. 'What sort of medicine are you currently working in?'

'Insurance.' A slight line of tension stiffened his jaw.

Astonishment filled Jess. Insurance medicine was general check-ups, giving second opinions for claims. It was dry and dull and involved no real patient care. It was the total opposite of the sort of medicine David practised. 'So you're no longer dashing off to far-flung places?'

'No.' The word came out harsh and abrupt, cutting the conversation off completely.

Jess felt as if she'd been hit by an arctic blast. The deep tension lines reappeared on his face and his stance became rigid. It was as if he'd hung up a *DO NOT ENTER* sign, and created a no-go force-field.

All her earlier apprehension returned in a rush. So much for making polite conversation. They'd hardly started and he'd shut down as tight as a drum. Just great. David had left her with a prickly, moody doctor. It was going to be a long three months.

The familiar tightening gripped Alex's chest. Hell! One innocent question from David's practice nurse and his emotions unravelled.

He saw the surprise and shock on her face at his harsh, 'No.' He should explain, but right now he couldn't go there.

Too hard. Far too hard.

And what could he really say? Words didn't help. His son was dead and time didn't heal.

But Jess had only been trying to be friendly. Jess, with the large chocolate-brown eyes that crinkled with laughter. Jess, whose stray strands of chestnut hair caressed her face in the sea breeze, making his fingers itch to tuck them back behind her ears and feel the softness of her skin.

And her crazy dress code of bright-coloured overalls that would suit a clown more than a nurse. She had no right to look so sweet and sexy all at the same time, stirring up feelings he'd buried long ago.

Damn David for rushing off to the Pacific like that. Pulling him in to run the practice at a moment's notice. He should have said no. He should have stayed in Melbourne, doing the mind-numbing but safe medical insurance work he'd done for the past two years.

But David was like a brother, and no was never an option.

However, David had *never* mentioned Jess. His last practice nurse had been fifty and a grandmother. Alex hadn't been able to hide his surprise when David had introduced Jess. The wariness on her heart-shaped face had told him she'd seen it.

And he'd seen her sadness when the Parkinsons had left.

So neither of them was happy. It was going to be a long three months.

'And, of course, on top of our commitment to the Roseport community, right now we have an influx of summer tourists, which doubles the population.'

Jess had spent the last thirty minutes giving Alex a brief rundown of the programmes and general clinic business of the Health Centre. It had been good to concentrate on work for half an hour. Work was the one stable thing in her life at the moment. Home was chaotic as she took a crash course of on-the-job training in learning to be a mother.

And concentrating on work rather than the strong-jawed man in front of her was the only sensible thing to do. She would ignore the shimmering feelings that whizzed through her whenever Alex looked at her.

OK, so David wouldn't be here for a while, but there was no reason why work couldn't continue to be her solid, dependable rock. A refuge from her private life. Alex Fitzwilliam wouldn't change that.

She pushed away the niggling thoughts that he might not be up to the job. David would never have left his practice in unsafe hands. But working in insurance medicine? She hoped Alex had the patient skills for the diverse medicine Roseport threw out. Only time would tell.

'Do the tourists tend to get themselves into trouble?' Alex leaned back in his chair, his shirt stretching tautly across his chest.

For a brief moment Jess's mesmerised gaze followed his fluid movement. She fleetingly wondered how his abdominal muscles would feel under her fingers. Horrified at her blatant staring and unwelcome thoughts, she pulled her mind back to Alex's question. 'Trouble tends to find them. Anything from car accidents, near drownings to general cuts and scratches. As the clinic is so close to the main tourist beach we've set up a—'

A piercing high-pitched sound screeched around the office. Jess raced for the door.

'What the hell is that?' Alex followed her.

'It means an emergency at the beach. The lifesavers activate it when they need medical back-up. Come on.' She ran down the corridor into the treatment room, grabbing the emergency packs. 'Here.' She tossed one pack to Alex. 'I'll bring the other one.'

'Anna,' she called to the receptionist. 'Switch the phones to message bank and bring the mobile. We might need you.'

'Will do.' Anna calmly activated the emergency procedure.

Jess dashed across the road, assuming Alex was following her.

His deep voice suddenly sounded in her ear. 'Where to now?' He looked along the wide expanse of beach.

'There.' Jess pointed to the lifeguard waving frantically at them.

A group of people had gathered, shock and disbelief marking their faces.

'Let us through. We're the medical team. Move aside.' Alex's voice boomed out in a commanding tone and the people responded.

Jess relaxed slightly. It looked as if Dr Fitzwilliam was happy to take charge.

They reached the lifeguard. 'What happened?'

Jess heard their voices merge as they spoke together.

'Three teenagers were digging a sand cave and it's collapsed on one of them, burying him.' The lifeguard's face was blanched white. 'He's been under almost three minutes.'

Bile rose in Jess's throat. Three minutes under sand and the kid would be asphyxiated—let alone the myriad of crush injuries he might sustain. 'Anna, call Medflight *now*.' She turned to the lifeguard. 'Get the portable defibrillator from the clubhouse.' She turned and dropped to her knees to help Alex.

He'd whipped his jacket off and was down in one of

the large holes. He looked at one of the terrified teenagers whose mate was under the sand. 'Where would his head have been?'

'He was connecting these two holes.' The teenager's voice was barely audible in his shock.

'Right.' He picked up a shovel and made three deep digs. 'Jess?' He called her over. 'You dig with your hands after I've removed this sand with the shovel. We can't risk putting a shovel through his face.'

Time moved slowly, yet far too quickly. Every second counted if this boy was to be pulled out alive. The surge of adrenaline inside Jess made her hands dig frantically, trying to feel something other than sand.

She dug down and touched material. 'I've got him!' She tried to pull him out, but the sand and the weight of the boy were too much for her.

Alex hollowed out the sand, locating the boy's head and shoulders. In a calm yet commanding voice he spoke to the friend. 'Put your hands under his left shoulder. On my count of three you pull with all your might.'

Alex gripped under the boy's right armpit. 'One, two, three.' They pulled the lad out from the sand, white and unconscious.

Jess placed her fingers on his carotid pulse. Nothing. Not even a faint beat. Dread filled her. She looked straight at Alex. His eyes were now dark with worry, confirming what they had both feared.

She spoke first. 'No pulse.'

'You breathe him; I'll compress.' Alex's words formalised her own plan.

She immediately cleared his airway of sand. Tilting

his head back and keeping her hand on his jaw, she applied cricoid pressure to his throat to prevent regurgitation from his stomach. He didn't need aspirate pneumonia as well. She placed the Laerdal pocket mask over his mouth and placed her lips around the one-way value, blowing her breath into his lungs. Years of training sounded in her head. *Five breaths in, then check the pulse.*

As she drew in her next breath she turned her head to check for the rise and fall of the boy's chest. She checked for his pulse, but knew it unlikely to be there based on breathing alone.

Nothing.

'Start compressions.'

Alex's hands crossed on the lad's chest. Then, with his arms straight and strong, he started compressing the chest one third down, in an attempt to massage the heart to start.

His firm voice counted. 'One, two, three, four, five.'

Jess counted with him in her head. On the fifth compression she blew in a breath. *One, two, three, four, five. Breathe.* The noise of the beach receded as she focussed on the count, willing this boy's heart to start.

Alex's arms pumped rhythmically. With confidence. *He's done this a lot of times before.* The thought raced through Jess's brain, one consoling thought in the middle of a crisis. Cardio-pulmonary resuscitation was something all medical staff knew, but it didn't necessarily mean they used it all that often. And probably never in insurance medicine.

'Oh, my God! Christopher!' The anguish in the voice sliced through Jess.

She glanced up. Fear, stark and raw, marked the woman's face. 'He's my son. Will he be all right?'

Jess looked at Alex, willing him to reply, but he continued counting, ignoring the woman. In fact, he looked away.

His lack of action forced her to respond. She swallowed hard. 'We're doing our best.' The words sounded hollow to her own ears, lacking the reassurance the woman so desperately craved.

'Where the hell is the lifeguard?' Alex growled. 'Check for a pulse.' The clipped words betrayed his anxiety. 'I need a time-check.'

'Four minutes.' Jess's fingers probed against the boy's carotid artery. Nothing. She shook her head.

Alex mouthed an expletive and continued compressions.

'Move back, everyone, and let me through.' The lifeguard arrived with the defibrillator.

'You.' Alex nodded towards the lifeguard.

'Eric.'

'Eric, take over the breathing from Jess. Jess, you compress and I'll defibrillate. Right—on my count. One, two, three.'

Jess moved in next to Alex, her arms brushing his as she took over the compressions.

'Jess.' Anna's worried voice called to her. 'The helicopter is on its way.'

She nodded her thanks.

Alex turned on the defibrillator, then attached the defibrillator pads and ECG lines to Christopher's chest.

The machine beeped. Alex placed the paddles on Christopher's chest. 'Stand clear.'

Jess and Eric leaned back. Jess caught Alex's look of apprehension. They needed to get this boy's heart started to avoid brain damage.

To save his life.

The defibrillator surged two hundred joules into Christopher. All eyes stared at the monitor screen. A flat line travelled across it.

The furrows on Alex's brow deepened as he pressed the full energy button. Three hundred and sixty joules. 'Stand clear.' His voice held a slight tremble.

Christopher's body jolted when the electrical current whipped through him.

The monitor displayed a flat line.

'Breathe him now, and start compressions.' Alex's command held despair and frustration. A fourteen-year-old boy lay dying before them.

Jess blocked out the sobs of Christopher's mother. She had to concentrate on the job and not let the emotion get to her. That could happen later. If sheer human force of will could bring Christopher back he would be alive.

She started compressions. She glanced over to see Alex, standing stock-still, his face almost white. Why wasn't he putting in an IV? 'Alex!' Panic gripped her.

He turned at her call, his eyes momentarily blank and unseeing before they cleared with a jolt. 'Where's the saline?'

'In the red box.' She inclined her head towards the container she'd carried to the beach. 'There's adrenaline as well. Breathe!'

Eric blew air into Christopher's mouth.

Alex started towards the box. 'Right—thanks. Got it.' He pulled a ludicrously bright tourniquet from the box and clicked it in place around the boy's leg, looking for a vein to insert the IV, his fingers moving deftly over the pale skin. 'Time-check.'

'Eight minutes.' Jess watched, praying he'd find a vein, knowing it wouldn't be easy. How long since he'd had to do this on a compromised patient? He wouldn't face this sort of trauma during medical insurance claims. That thought kept nagging at her. He seemed to lurch from total control to a moment of sheer terror. Coldness filled her when she thought of his blank stare.

Her arms started burning as she continued cardiac compressions. She counted out loud, nodding at the white-faced Eric, reassuring him that his technique was good.

Alex ripped the cannulae packet open. With a slightly trembling hand he inserted a cannula and drew back the trocar. Blood raced in.

'Well done.' Jess breathed out the words.

'Thanks.' His mouth remained a grim line. He connected the IV. 'I'll take over the compressions; you give the adrenaline.'

'Let's swap on five.' Relief filled her. The doctor in charge was back in control. She appreciated his teamwork approach. Her arms couldn't have held out with the same intensity of action for much longer.

Shoving the bag of intravenous saline into the arms of an onlooker, Jess instructed, 'Hold it high over your shoulder.' She reached into the box for the adrenaline and snapped off the top of the glass ampoule. Flicking the plastic cover off the needle, she withdrew the clear liquid into the syringe. 'One milligram IV every three minutes?' She automatically confirmed the dose with Alex.

'Correct.' His strong arms continued to pump Christopher's chest, trying to circulate the blood and keep some oxygen in his body. 'Give it now, so it increases the blood supply to the heart. Then defibrillate with three hundred and sixty joules. It's *got* to work.'

The desperation in his voice tore at her, escalating her own panic that this boy might die. That no matter what they did they might not be able to save him. She looked up to see a line of sweat beads on his forehead and his emerald eyes dark with fear for Christopher. Fear mixed in with another emotion she didn't have time to decipher.

Plunging the syringe into the rubber bung of the IV, she administered the adrenaline. Then she picked up the defibrillator paddles and laid them on Christopher's chest. 'Stand clear.'

Releasing the charge, she glued her gaze to the monitor. The green line flickered. Then flattened.

'Do it again!' Alex hollered the instruction, his voice frantic. Time was against them.

The machine beeped. 'Stand clear.' She released the charge.

The green line leapt as a T-wave appeared, followed by a P, Q, R, S and another T. Sinus rhythm.

'We've got him back.' Jess wanted to high five, even though she knew the situation could change in a heartbeat. Behind her she could hear Christopher's mother sobbing with relief.

'Thank God.' For a brief moment Alex seemed to

slump as if he was winded, his face paling under his tan. Then almost as quickly his shoulders straightened. 'Jess, he's not breathing on his own. You bag him with the air viva.' He grimaced. 'Where's the bloody helicopter? We'll have to intubate if they don't get here soon.'

Jess understood the grimace. Christopher was alive but it was a precarious hold on life. He might have brain damage; he might have another cardiac arrest. He needed to be in Intensive Care.

'You'll talk to his mother now?' Jess squeezed the green bag, giving air to Christopher.

Alex stilled. His shoulders went rigid and his jaw tightened.

What was going on here? He *should* speak with the mother.

Suddenly, the deafening noise of the Med-E-Vac helicopter filled the air as it landed.

'Time for us to hand over to the Med-E-Vac team. Our bit is over,' Alex yelled into her ear as the team ran across towards them.

Later, Jess stood watching the helicopter recede into the distance. She could feel her legs start to shake as the trembling raced through her body. After-shocks. She wrapped her arms around herself to try and steady the shivers.

'Are you all right?' Alex's baritone voice sounded concerned.

She gripped herself harder. 'That was the hardest thing I've had to do in a long time.'

'Yeah. It was a hell of a welcome to Roseport.' He gave a wry smile.

Jess's stomach flipped over and warmth spread

through her. It must be part of the post-trauma shock. 'I thought we were going to lose him.'

'So did I.' Pain lanced his face.

She thought back to when he'd seemed to go blank. 'But we didn't lose him.'

'No. *He* was lucky.' A sigh shuddered through him.

Jess instinctively put her hand on his arm.

He stiffened at her touch and a desperate sorrow slashed his face.

Jess recognised that sort of pain. She'd felt it when her sister Elly had died. 'It's my turn to ask if you're all right.'

'I'm fine.' He stepped back sharply, breaking the contact. 'We need to get back to the clinic; we'll have patients waiting. Come on.' He picked up the emergency packs and started striding down the beach.

Stunned at his abrupt departure, Jess had no option but to follow.

Back at the clinic, Alex downed three glasses of cold water. Sweat poured off him. He ripped off his tie and unbuttoned his shirt, trying to cool down. Breathing deeply, he concentrated on slowing his racing heart-rate down to normal. They'd saved the teenager. Christopher hadn't died.

Jess had seen to that.

He'd frozen. Images of Nick had swamped him. Images of his own son lying, dying, in front of him.

He should have spoken to Christopher's mother—but her shock and grief, so raw, so familiar, had rendered him mute. The combination of surprise and censure on Jess's face had cut him deeply. Should he even be *trying* to practise medicine? He belonged with safe insurance check-ups. No life-and-death decisions there. No opportunities to relive past horrors.

Bloody David. He shouldn't have listened to him. David had convinced him to come down here as a way of getting back into mainstream medicine. He'd lured him to Roseport with promises of rural medicine and the quiet life. Not kids dying on beaches. He needed to leave. He couldn't go through that again.

But he'd given his word to David. Mates didn't let each other down.

And then there was Jess.

If he left Jess would look at him with those large brown eyes. And for some reason he didn't want to see disappointment and breach of faith reflected back to him. For some reason that mattered. It mattered a lot.

And that in itself stressed the hell out of him.

CHAPTER TWO

THE rest of the day passed without incident. Jess had been busy with a diabetic clinic, and apart from Alex asking a couple of questions she hadn't seen him. Part of her wanted to get more glimpses of him, hoping to catch another one of his smiles.

Gathering up her files, she wondered how the patients were finding him. Moody? Prickly? Helpful? She'd seen so many different sides to him in their first two hours together she was confused about the type of doctor he really was.

She kept reliving that moment on the beach when she'd asked him if he was all right.

She tried to rationalise his abrupt manner. They hardly knew each other, so why would he open up to her? And yet he'd genuinely sounded concerned when he'd asked how *she* was.

Why couldn't he accept the same courtesy? He'd jumped back from her touch so quickly it was as if he thought her toxic.

But it wasn't just her. His behaviour with people seemed strained, and he'd avoided talking to

Christopher's mother. That rankled. He should have spoken to her, no matter how hard.

Her watch beeped. 'Five-thirty.' She had to get moving to pick Woody up on time from the crèche. After years of staying at work late, she wasn't used to having to leave right on time, so had bought a watch that chimed just to keep her on track.

Running down the corridor, files in her arms, she dumped them on the table behind Anna. 'I promise I'll file them in the morning.'

Anna smiled. 'No worries. But I thought that new watch was going to solve you being late?'

'I think I need to set it to go off every ten minutes from five o'clock.' Jess gave a wry smile and then, trying to sound casual, said, 'How's the new doctor settling in?'

Anna gave a wicked grin. 'He's gorgeous to look at, that's for sure.'

'If you like that sort of look.' Jess tried to sound off-hand. She was still struggling with the fact that Alex Fitzwilliam could send a wall of heat through her with one look. She didn't want that sort of attraction.

Anna continued, 'He doesn't say much, does he? He's sure not outgoing, like David. Funny that, seeing as they're such good mates.'

'He might just take a bit of time to warm up to us, that's all.' Jess wanted to shake herself. Why was she defending a man she hardly knew?

'Probably.' Anna gave Jess a gentle shove. 'Go and get Woody, and give him a hug from me.'

'Thanks, Anna. See you tomorrow.'

Jess ran out to her car and drove the short distance to the crèche.

'Jess! Jess!'

As she walked up the path, her little redheaded boy threw himself against her legs. A rush of love shot through her. She stooped down and pulled him, wriggling and full of energy, into her arms.

'Hello, sweetheart. How are you?' She returned his body-slam hug and swung Woody in her arms, resting him on her hip. She headed over to the office to speak with his carer.

'Hi, Jess.' Helen reached for the daily report outlining Woody's activities for the day. 'He's had a wonderful day.' She handed her the sheet. 'I think he's settling in now, and feeling much more comfortable with us.'

'Thanks, Helen.' Jess smiled gratefully. 'I was starting to despair that he'd ever be happy here.' She thought back to the mornings when the carers had had to pry a screaming, terrified child from her arms. She would arrive at work a trembling mess and have to telephone the crèche to see if he had calmed down. Before two months ago, he'd never even been to a crèche.

Poor kid. His life had changed as dramatically as hers.

'Woody's had a lot of adjustments to make in a short time. Just take each day as it comes. You're doing fine, Jess. Stop trying so hard and take some time to enjoy him.' Helen ruffled Woody's hair. 'Bye-bye, Woody.'

'Bye-bye.' At twenty-two months, Woody's vocabulary expanded every day.

Jess strapped him into the car seat and kissed the top of his head. 'We're going home now.'

The next two hours flew by, with making dinner, playtime, bath, bedtime stories and settling Woody into his cot. Jess loved this time with Woody. A time when they didn't have to rush and she could give him plenty of love and attention.

Snuggled up against his bear and his rabbit, Woody looked peaceful and content.

Jess's heart went out to him. He would never remember his parents and their wonderful love for him.

Matey, you've got all my love. I hope it's enough.

She sighed and walked downstairs. Fatigue pulled at every part of her. She poured herself a glass of wine, then sat on the balcony and looked out into the night. The lights of Roseport twinkled at her from down the hill.

She thought of the tiny balcony she'd used to stand on in her flat in Melbourne to stare out at the lights. A *lot* more lights.

Her life in Melbourne seemed a million years ago. Her life with Robert.

She sighed. How had she been so stupid as to waste three years of her life on that man? How could she have been blind to who he really was? She'd got it *so* wrong.

It had taken Elly and Patrick's death to make her see clearly. Robert hadn't loved her. She'd been convenient, the right type of woman for a new consultant. He certainly hadn't wanted her if she came with a child.

She walked back into the house and shivered, a sense of emptiness chilling her. Sometimes living in Elly and Patrick's house was more than she could bear. Their presence was imprinted on everything, making their absence keenly felt. But moving Woody so soon after their death wasn't something she wanted to do. So she'd put up with her ghosts a little longer.

She turned on the local radio station and Elvis filled the room with 'Are you Lonesome Tonight?' With half a moan and a laugh she spun the dial and settled on classical music with no lyrics.

Am I lonesome? She breathed in deeply as a barren ache caught in her chest.

She gave herself a shake. She shouldn't be lonely. Work kept her busy, and Anna and the Parkinsons were friendly and supportive. And Woody gave her unconditional love.

But was it enough? She'd never pictured herself living this type of life. Alone.

Switching off the lights, she walked past the balcony window and looked out. One light burned in the Parkinsons' window. Alex was still up.

An image of sea-green eyes and chiselled cheeks flashed into her mind. And that delectable smile. Although infrequent, when he did smile her world seemed to light up.

But Alex Fitzpatrick was a conundrum. Pleasant and outgoing one minute, closed up the next. And he was only in Roseport for a short-term stay. He wouldn't be around for the long haul.

This time she had more at stake. Woody must never be hurt by her poor choice of men. He needed stability and love.

Right now she needed to channel her energies into creating a loving home for Woody. Together, the two of them would be just fine.

* * *

Roseport didn't need traffic lights. Not for eleven months of the year, anyway.

But in January tourists clogged the roads. Facing a stop light, Jess drummed her fingers against the steering wheel as a stream of early-morning traffic passed her. Whatever had happened to sleeping in on holiday? Why weren't these people still in their beds, instead of making her late for work?

And why on a Thursday, the busiest day of her week? She had a new mother's group, and an asthma clinic. And somewhere in between that she had to create a reason to watch Alex in action with the patients. She needed to know that he was able to cope with general practice. She didn't doubt his medical knowledge. It was the nuances of handling the patients that worried her. Especially after he'd ignored Christopher's mother.

She glanced down at the huge wet stain on her front. She'd hoped the early heat of the day would dry it before she got to work. Just as she'd been getting ready to leave, Woody had managed to find the hose. But it was Jess who'd got wet. The unpredictability of their morning routine was something she still struggled with. At least this morning she didn't have Vegemite on her shoulder.

She sighed. No doubt Alex Fitzwilliam would be dressed in another Italian suit and she would feel like a complete frump.

The traffic cleared, she pulled onto the main road, and five minutes later she walked into the clinic.

'Good morning.' Alex stood in the waiting area and gave her a friendly smile.

Jess's voice caught in her throat—along with her breath. The designer suit was nowhere to be seen. In its place Alex wore an open-neck linen shirt, the sky-blue colour deepening his sea-green eyes. Stone-coloured shorts moulded to his hips and finished just above his knees, exposing strong, muscular, tanned legs. And, to complete the smart-casual look, his feet resided in brown boat shoes. No man should be allowed to look so gorgeous at ten past nine in the morning. Not when she looked half drowned.

'Did you walk through a sprinkler?' His look lingered on her soggy shirt for a moment, then he lifted his gaze, his eyes dancing with suppressed laughter and a hint of something else she couldn't pick.

Jess found her voice. 'You could say that. Sorry I'm late—the traffic was dreadful.'

Alex laughed, a deep, warm laugh that sent a thrill quivering through her.

How could her body betray her like this?

'The traffic? It takes longer just to drive to my local milk bar in Melbourne than it takes to get around this town.'

'So? I've acclimatised quickly.' She grinned, enjoying the banter. Enjoying talking with a relaxed Alex rather than the buttoned-up man she'd met yesterday. 'Looks like you have too.'

'Yeah, well, the suit didn't really fit in Roseport, did it? Any more beach emergencies and it would have ended up stone-washed from the sand.'

Again he smiled, and her knees went to jelly. She struggled to kickstart her brain. It was time to bring this conversation around to work. Work was safe. 'I better get going, or my new mothers' group will think I'm not coming.'

She turned to walk down the corridor.

'Jess?'

She turned back. 'Yes?'

'I rang the Royal Children's Hospital last night. Christopher is breathing on his own.'

'That's marvellous news.' A tiny spark of pleasure zipped thought her, relaxing her concerns. He'd followed up on his patient. She hadn't been certain he would.

'Yes, it is.' For a moment he looked uncomfortable, and then he seemed to take in a deep breath. 'You did really well yesterday and I should have thanked you.'

'No need. We both did our jobs.'

'You did more than that, Jess, and you know it. I just want you to know I appreciate it, and I don't plan on freezing again. Put it down to first-day nerves.' He moved towards his office. 'I'll catch you later in the day, at the practice meeting.' He closed the door behind him.

First-day nerves? Jess didn't think so. But Alex was good at wall-building. He'd just acknowledged his freezing, thanked her, and then in a very polite way prevented her from pushing him any further to find out the reason why.

So she would just have to observe him in action, as she'd planned, to see if her gut instincts were right or wrong.

An hour later, after cuddling six babies and having reassured each of their mothers that everyone was healthy, Jess was buzzed by Anna.

'Mr O'Grady's come in. He wants to see you. Do you have some time?'

'No problem. I'll see him now.' She walked down the corridor to collect her patient, grabbing his file on the way.

'How are you. Mr O?' Jess extended her arm to the usually spry elderly gentleman who struggled to get up from his chair.

'Not the best today, dear. Maisy brought me in. Said I should come and see Dr David. But Anna says he's not here, so I thought I'd talk to you.'

Jess followed him down the corridor, worried by his unusually wobbly gait. She sat him down in her office. 'So what's the problem?'

'Well, I just feel crook, Sis.'

Jess smiled. 'Exactly how do you feel crook?'

'I feel like I'm going to be sick, and I've had the runs.'

Gastro had been going around. But, just in case it wasn't that, Jess probed a bit more. 'Any other symptoms?'

He hesitated just a moment, his rheumy eyes clouding. 'I can't see as well. Maisy had to drive home from Tangawallah yesterday.'

'When you say you can't see, what exactly do you mean?' Jess's mind started to run over possibilities.

'Blurry, out of focus.'

'How long have you been feeling like this?' She wrapped the blood pressure cuff around his arm.

'Since Christmas.'

She put the stethoscope in her ears. 'Three weeks is a long time to be feeling poorly.' She pumped the cuff and listened to the slow booming noise as the blood flowed through the arteries against the pressure cuff.

Pulling the stethoscope out of her ears, she said, 'Your BP is fine, so that's good.' Her fingers located the pulse on his wrist, which was reasonably regular considering he had atrial fibrillation.

'Did anything happen around Christmas? I know you went to see your daughter in early December.'

'I did get a nasty skin infection a couple of weeks ago. Luckily Maisy had some antibiotics, so I took them and it cleared up.'

'Mr O, taking other people's prescription medication isn't a good idea. It can cause problems with the tablets you are already on.' Jess flipped open his history and scanned his list of medication. 'When you say your vision is blurry, do things look yellow as well?'

He started in surprise. 'Yes, they do.'

'Wait here, Mr O. You're about to meet Dr Fitzwilliam.'

Jess headed down to knock on Alex's office door, trying not to hum. She had just found her reason for seeing Alex in action. She met him in the corridor. 'I have a patient who I think is digoxin toxic, but I'm not certain. He's been taking his wife's antibiotics.'

'Any arrhythmias?'

'I haven't done an ECG yet. But the symptoms are more non-cardiac. He's nauseated, he's got diarrhoea, and yellow vision. Do you have time to see him now?'

'Sure. Is he in your office?'

She nodded, and moved to follow him down the corridor, but Alex paused and she almost barrelled into him.

'Sorry.' She teetered on the balls of her feet, suddenly

flustered by his closeness and the scent of his woodsy aftershave.

He smiled a teasing grin, white teeth flashing against a tanned face, and put his hands on her shoulders to steady her.

Delicious tendrils shot through her, weaving their magic, bringing dormant feelings back to life.

He dropped his hands and with a gentle push on the small of her back said, 'After you.'

'Thanks.' She walked back to her office feeling foolish, gauche, and slightly disappointed that she couldn't watch him walk down the corridor and see how the cotton twill of his shorts moved across his buttocks.

'Mr O, this is Dr Fitzwilliam.' Jess introduced the pair.

Alex leaned forward and extended his hand to the elderly man. 'Pleased to meet you, Mr O'Grady.' He pulled up a chair next to the patient so they were both at the same level. 'Jess tells me you've not been feeling so well.'

'Bit of gastro that won't shift.'

'We're thinking it might be more than that. Can you tell me the name of the antibiotics you were taking?'

Mr O'Grady rubbed his forehead. 'Clairo-something.'

Alex nodded. 'Clarithromycin?'

'Yeah, that sounds right. Would they be causing the trouble?'

'Combined with the tablets you're taking for your heart, yes. Those antibiotics mean you're getting more digoxin—those little blue tablets—than you need. That's why everything looks a bit yellow to you.'

'Well, I'll be. Can you stop me feeling so bloody nauseous?'

Alex smiled and gave the man's shoulder a quick squeeze. 'That I can do. But it's going to involve a few days in the hospital at Ryeton. We need to put you on a drip and change your medication, and then monitor your heartbeat.'

Mr O'Grady's shoulders slumped. 'There's no other way? It's just Maisy doesn't cope alone too well.'

Concern creased Alex's brow. 'I'm afraid hospital is the place you have to be. We need to monitor you. You don't want your heart going into a funny beat, do you? That would worry Maisy more, wouldn't it?'

He turned to Jess. 'Is there any way Mrs O'Grady could go to Ryeton? Or can someone stay with her?'

Relief filled Jess. Alex was treating Mr O'Grady like a real person, not just a patient with a medical condition. Perhaps yesterday had just been a blip.

She gave their patient a smile. 'Mr O'Grady, I can contact the bowls club. I'm sure Elsie Griffiths would be happy to spend a couple of nights at your place, keeping Maisy company.'

'Would you, dear? That would be great—thank you.' For the first time since arriving Mr O'Grady relaxed, as if a weight had been lifted off his shoulders.

Alex turned back to his patient. 'In a couple of days you'll be feeling a lot better, and you should be home by the weekend. I'll organise a dosette for you, so your daily medications are all laid out and there can be no mistakes.'

'Thanks, Doc. I was worried about seeing a new doc, but you're all right.' The old man gave a tired smile.

Jess bit her lip so she didn't laugh at Alex being

damned by faint praise. But Mr O was right; Alex *was* 'all right'. 'I'll get Anna to contact Ryeton hospital transport.'

'Good. Thanks.' Alex nodded as he reached for the writing pad to write a referral letter to Ryeton.

'I'll ring Maisy as well, Mr O, and hopefully in a couple of hours you'll be tucked up under those pretty blue eiderdowns in the medical ward.' She gave her patient a reassuring smile.

'Thanks, Sis, I appreciate your help.'

Jess left the room feeling a lot more confident about Alex. Her gut instinct had been wrong and it was OK to admit that. Sometimes she got it wrong. Not often, but sometimes. Perhaps it *had* been first-day nerves after all.

It took more than an hour, but Jess waved Mr O'Grady off around two o'clock. She'd settled him in the treatment room and had checked on him in between her asthma clinic patients.

Her stomach growled. Lunch hadn't happened, and she determinedly walked towards the kitchen for the ham sandwich she'd thrown together this morning with Woody's 'help'. One piece of bread had lumps of butter on it and the other a large hole. Thank goodness for cling wrap. Funny how things like making a quick sandwich took on a whole new meaning when a toddler was involved.

'Jess!' Anna called her.

Jess recognised that voice. It meant drop everything and come to Reception. Sighing, she walked back to the front of the building to see Meredith Walker holding her sobbing four-year-old son with one arm and pressing a hankie to his knee. Anna would have taken one look at the blood and called Jess.

'What happened, Jake? Did you fall off the monkey bars?'

The usually happy Jake looked up at her through watery eyes and hiccoughed.

'Come on, then. You bring Mum down to my special room.'

Jake visited quite often, as Meredith seemed to panic whenever there was blood.

'Sorry, Jess. There was just so much blood—and he might need stitches, do you think?' Meredith's voice quavered as she sat Jake on the treatment room couch.

'Let's take a look.' She handed Jake a lollipop before putting on a pair of gloves. She removed the hankie. Bits of gravel clung to broken skin. She carefully washed away the blood with normal saline and cleaned the wound.

Jake squirmed.

'Did you make a hole in the ground when you fell, Jake?'

The boy looked at her and sniffed. 'No, silly. The ground hurt me.'

Jess smiled. 'It's just superficial, Meredith. It's bleeding a lot but it isn't deep. No stitches required. I've covered it with a waterproof dressing which you can take off in three days.'

'Thanks, Jess.' Meredith looked relieved.

'No problems.' Jess ripped off the gloves and dropped them into the bin. 'I'm running a basic first aid course soon. How about you put your name down and join the group? I'd love to have you in the class. Sign up with Anna on your way out.'

Jess caught sight of Alex walking past. 'Excuse me just a minute, Meredith.'

She walked over to the door. 'Alex?'

He turned at her voice and smiled. Again Jess marvelled at how relaxed he was today compared with yesterday. His body moved fluidly, no sign of tension, and it made her increasingly aware of him. Making her heart beat more erratically each time she saw him.

'Come and meet Jake Walker. He's our resident walking disaster zone. He's in every second week.'

He moved towards the open door, and then stopped stock-still. His shoulders emanated tension as his gaze rested on the dark-haired Jake, who sat contentedly on the other side of the large room, eating his lollipop.

He quickly stepped away from the door, back into the corridor.

Startled, Jess followed him out of the room. 'Alex?'

'What's he here for?' His voice was sharp.

'He fell over and cut his knee.'

'Does it need stitches?' The clipped words shot into the air like pellets from a gun.

His questions hammered her and she struggled to work out what was going on. Why the abrupt change in his manner? 'No, it was just a superficial wound.'

'You've cleaned it up and put on a dressing?'

'Yes, but—'

'So he doesn't need to see a doctor?'

Her shock and surprise gave way to justification.

'No, but I thought that you should meet him and his mum because he will probably be coming in again while you're here and—'

'Jess, I'm busy.' His curt voice sliced into her. 'I have a waiting room full of patients who need to see me. You're more than qualified to deal with this and I don't have time to be social with patients I might not ever need to meet.' He turned abruptly and walked away.

She stood for a moment, opening and closing her mouth, wishing for a line to hurl at his retreating back. But her brain was numb from his unexpected reaction.

Was this the difference between country and city medicine? In Roseport the medical staff were part of the community; they lived amongst their patients. Meeting and greeting was part of life.

But blaming his reaction on the city/country difference was too easy, and she wasn't certain it was right.

He'd been so kind, gentle and considerate with Mr O'Grady. His behaviour just now didn't make sense. All he'd had to do was go and say hello, ruffle Jake's hair and introduce himself to Meredith.

How hard was that?

Yesterday he hadn't spoken to Christopher's mother. Today he wouldn't greet a mother and child.

Something wasn't right.

She sighed. She was no closer to understanding what made Alex Fitzwilliam tick. Beneath all that tanned skin, taut muscle and broad shoulders was a maelstrom of emotions that erupted at different times—sometimes calm, sometimes stormy, and sometimes so damn sexy that it confused the hell out of her.

But this sort of thing couldn't go on.

The next time he reacted like this with a patient she wouldn't let him walk away. Next time he would have to explain. Next time she was going to drag down those walls he'd built up around himself and find out what was hidden behind them.

CHAPTER THREE

ALEX poured himself a glass of wine and walked outside to sit on the Parkinsons' deck. He preferred it out here, away from all the family photos scattered on every surface in the living room.

David's house screamed happy families. He was tempted to turn the photos face down, but the cleaning lady would just right them all.

He sipped the fruity Sauvignon Blanc and looked out across the bay. The turquoise water shimmered, reflecting the rays from the setting sun. Rust-red cliffs glowed, deepening the ochre.

He sighed. He'd got through day two. Just. Sort of. Only eighty-eight days to go.

He'd actually enjoyed the variety of patients he'd seen. Roseport had a large retired population with varied health needs. But he'd also treated some teenagers and a baby. For the first time in a couple of years he'd really used his skills. He'd had to think, analyse. He loved the thrill of connecting all the diagnostic parts.

But when he'd seen that dark-haired kid, so similar in looks and age to Nick, and so full of life, his heart had hammered so hard against his ribs, the blood had roared in his ears and he'd known he had to get out of that room.

And Jess had borne the brunt of his post-traumatic reaction.

God, he hated that term. Post-traumatic stress disorder. What about 'heart-ripped-out-of your-chest' disorder or 'kids-don't-deserve-to-die' syndrome.

Jess would be thinking David had left his practice in the hands of a lunatic. He'd told Jess he wouldn't freeze again. And he hadn't. But he'd ducked the issue.

And the gorgeous Jess didn't deserve to be hit with his problems. An image of her in her damp T-shirt filled his mind and his groin tightened. He'd had to work extremely hard at not openly staring at her this morning when she'd arrived. It had been a long time since a woman had stirred his interest, and Jess had curves that screamed to be explored.

But he had to work with her for another eighty-eight days. And he wasn't in Roseport to race off with the practice nurse. Right now, she probably thought him erratic and moody. So tomorrow he was starting over. Tomorrow would be the first day of being in total control. And Jess would see a whole new side of him.

'All ready for the immunisation clinic?' Alex found Jess in the kitchen having a late lunch, eating a most unusual-looking sandwich. 'What happened? Did the dog get to it?'

Jess laughed—an infectious, joyous sound. 'It does look a bit like a dog's breakfast, doesn't it? But it tastes fine.' She put the sandwich down and brushed crumbs off her lips. 'I'm ready when you are.'

His gaze zeroed in on her unconscious action, staying fixed on her plump ruby lips. Lips that cried out to be explored, tasted and caressed. Heat surged inside him, shocking him with its intensity.

Her velvet-brown eyes widened as her gaze met his. Her tongue darted out and she licked the one remaining crumb, then swallowed.

A fire of longing exploded inside him.

Dragging on every ounce of will-power not to step forward and kiss her, he dragged his look away. *Focus on work.* 'I'm ready now.' The words rasped against his throat, coming out husky and deeper than normal.

Hell, he should just get a neon sign for his forehead saying 'sex-starved doctor'. And that wasn't the 'new side' of him that he'd had in mind to show Jess.

Jess stood up quickly, seeming flustered.

Just great. He'd freaked her out. Now she could add predator to lunatic.

Trying to sound completely professional and in control, he pulled his keys out of his pocket. 'I'll drive, if you like, and you can navigate. That'll help me find my way around—especially if I have a house call in the middle of the night.'

She looked uncomfortable. 'Sorry, but we'll need to go in separate cars in case you get a call-out. I have to be back in Roseport by five-thirty, so I can't get stranded in Veriparipna.'

'Hot date on a Friday night?' He tried to keep his voice light, hide the edge he felt. Of course she probably had a boyfriend. A beautiful, vivacious woman like her would. But he didn't like the idea one little bit.

For a brief moment she seemed discomposed. Then her head shot up and she laughed. 'Oh, yeah, absolute scorcher of a date.' Flinging her bag on her shoulder, she seemed to give herself a shake and stand slightly taller. 'You follow me, then. Getting to Veriparipna is pretty straightforward.'

The fifteen-minute trip up through towering gums and lush tree ferns passed quickly as Alex concentrated on the continuously winding road. Stunning in the sunshine, the road would be slick and treacherous in a rainstorm.

A faded sign heralded his arrival in Veriparipna. One general store, a pub in need of paint, one shuttered garage with an old sign advertising a petrol price that was truly historic, and a small weatherboard church.

Jess turned off the road and pulled up on the grass in front of the church.

For a brief moment he indulged himself, watching her get out and open the back of the station wagon. Today she wore a multi-coloured short skirt that flared as she walked, accentuating the swing of her hips and her sculptured legs.

Alex added great legs to his increasing list of things he'd noticed about Jess.

He quickly got out of his car and jogged over to her. 'Let me do that.' He pulled the refrigerated pack of immunisations out of the back of the clinic's car.

'Thanks.' She smiled a full smile, accentuating her high cheekbones.

The rays of her smile cascaded over Alex. His mother had been right. Good manners got rewards.

Jess opened the door with an enormous old-fashioned key and walked inside, her footsteps echoing around the empty hall. 'This is how we reach out to under-serviced communities. I applied for funding and we got it. Right now I'm working on making sure the local farmers are all up to date with tetanus shots, and trying to win over our "alternative" community who prefer more natural medicine.' She turned and gave him an earnest look. 'I know it doesn't look much, but it works.'

Alex looked around at the clean floorboards and up at the well-maintained roof. He spoke before thinking. 'It's a lot better than many places I've worked.'

A spark of interest flared in her eyes. 'Where have you worked?' Curiosity filled her voice as she started to set up tables.

He lifted one end of a table with her, ducking the question. 'Lots of places.'

'No, seriously. Where *have* you worked? You mentioned your first day that you'd worked overseas with David.'

He could hear firmness in her voice. She wasn't going to let the topic pass this time.

A band of muscle in his chest contracted slightly. He breathed in. He had to answer her. This was all part of showing her his 'new side'—the side where the past didn't swamp him. 'I've worked in India, Timor and Africa.'

'So Veriparipna church hall probably looks pretty

grand.' An understanding of Third World conditions shadowed her face.

He opened the fridge pack and looked down at the contents. Vials containing a variety of immunisations lay in neat rows. 'Yeah. We would have thrown a party if we'd received a pack like this.'

'I guess you learn to be inventive with what you have. I read once that in an emergency situation some medics built an operating area with large water containers because they had no building to use.'

'Yep, it's amazing what people can achieve in an emergency. But I wasn't doing crisis medicine and I wasn't in a war zone. I lived in villages.'

He concentrated on connecting needles to syringes, pleased to have something to do with his hands. 'It wasn't the gung-ho sort of stuff the media reports. It was primary health care with a tenth of what Australians take for granted when they visit the doctor.'

'Where was the last place you worked?'

He hesitated, and then forced the word out of his mouth. 'Africa.'

'Fantastic. What an experience to live and work in a place like that. How long ago were you there?' Her animated face shone with enthusiasm for the topic.

He hesitated. 'Two years.'

She paused from setting up and looked straight at him, her velvet eyes wide with interest. 'What brought you back to Australia and insurance medicine?'

Her questions hammered him. They were getting too close, too uncomfortable. 'It was time for a change.' Sweat started to break out on his forehead; his heart started to pound. He'd been polite, he'd answered her questions, but now he needed to change the topic. He looked at his watch. 'Time's getting on, Jess. Tell me, what's the plan for the afternoon?'

Three hours later, Jess dragged her concentration back to the paperwork in front of her. Her mind had been wandering all afternoon. Wandering to Alex, who was working on the other side of the hall, wearing a stethoscope with a tiny koala clinging to it, and charming all the mothers of the babies and toddlers who were being immunised.

She was sick of being told how 'gorgeous' the new doctor was. Did they all think she was blind? She spent most of her time deliberately *not* thinking about the way his reddish-blond chest hair curled out of his open-neck shirt, how his tanned legs with their taut muscles hinted at how hard and toned all his other muscles would be. And his mouth; those lips promised kisses of perfection.

Working alongside Alex increasingly rendered her a quivering mess of raging hormones and unwanted lust. But she was the mother of a toddler now. She couldn't be thinking like a teenage schoolgirl.

Except she was.

She sighed and looked at her watch. Only half an hour left of her working day. Then she was safely home, with an Alex-free weekend. A weekend of playing with Woody and trying to make up for being at work forty hours during the week.

'Earth to Jess.'

She looked up to see a group of young farmers in front of her. She'd been to the pub with them earlier in the week, to encourage them to come to the clinic today. She pushed thoughts of Alex away and concentrated on her patients.

'Right, guys. I need you to fill in these forms and then, seeing as I have you here, I'll take your blood pressure as well as giving you an injection.' She ignored the groans. Young men thought they were invincible, but if she had their attention she would at least be able to give them a quick health check.

The time flew past as she saw each of them. 'Roll up your sleeve, Phil.'

He grinned at her. 'If you insist, Jess. I can roll up other things too, you know.'

She couldn't resist smiling back at the cheeky farmer before she plunged the needle into his arm.

Ten minutes later she said goodbye to the last of the group.

Alex came over and joined her in packing up. 'All your farmers gone, have they? I had no idea country lads were such flirts.' His tone was mild, but there was something in his voice that made her look up into his face.

Those emerald eyes flecked with darker shards seemed to be even more green than usual. 'So we've finished for the day? I'll pack the car for you.' He began to clear away their things and disappeared out the side door.

Surprise rippled through her that he'd even noticed the flirting, let alone commented. For a brief moment she wondered what it would be like to flirt with Alex. But even though he'd opened up a bit today, telling her about Africa, he didn't seem the flirting type. Since his arrival he'd been polite, but slightly distant.

And yet at lunchtime in the staffroom she could have sworn he'd been staring at her. But that was probably her imagination. Part of her *wanted* him to stare at her, to find her attractive.

Robert's legacy of 'You can't possibly go out wearing that', and 'As a consultant, I need a partner who dresses impeccably, not like a gypsy,' had taken a bit of a toll on her confidence.

But what did it matter if Alex flirted or not? If he found her attractive or not? She wasn't in the market for a relationship. She had to protect Woody.

The door banged and a woman came in clutching a baby to her hip. In her other hand she gripped a sheaf of papers.

Jess stifled a sigh and took a surreptitious look at her watch. She didn't have much of a margin or she'd be late for the crèche. She hated being late to pick up Woody. He always started looking for her after his late-afternoon snack.

The baby's cheeks were flushed pink, matching her all-in-one suit. Mucous streamed out of her nose and she looked very lethargic. She didn't look well enough to have an immunisation injection today.

The woman wore large baggy pants with an Indian design and a woven vest. Colourful beads hung around her neck and her left ankle. Her long hair, streaked with grey, was pulled back and held in place with a piece of twine. Jess would bet her last dollar this woman was from the commune ten kilometres out of Veriparipna.

The commune Jess had been trying to make links with.

She stuck her hand forward. 'Hello, I'm Jess Henderson. How can I help you?'

'I'm Zondra Thompson, and I need to see the doctor so he can sign these school entry forms. We just moved here from the Daintree, and the school says the kids can't start until the papers are signed.'

Jess accepted the proffered papers and read them. They stated that the children weren't immunised against any childhood diseases. Occasionally children with an overriding illness weren't immunised, or children who experienced a severe reaction to the vaccine. And some families chose not to immunise their children—especially parents from the commune.

Jess silently groaned, forcing her face into an impassive mask. She knew from past experience that convincing some parents to have their children immunised took time and tact. For the children's health and safety she would find that time. But why did it have to happen late on a Friday afternoon?

The baby whimpered and laid her head on her mother's shoulder.

Jess's radar kicked in. The baby looked to be about nine months old, and not at all well. She put her hand out to touch the child's forehead. She was extremely hot to the touch and her breathing was noisy. Saliva ran down her cheek. 'Zondra, this little one doesn't look very well. How about Dr Fitzwilliam gives her a check-up and looks inside her ears while you're here?'

'Oh, she's just got a bit of a cold because she's cutting teeth. You know how they are in the first two years. They lurch from one cold to another.' The woman hitched the child further up her hip.

'I think it's more than a cold. She's pretty warm.' Jess gave what she hoped was an encouraging smile.

Zondra sniffed. 'It's hot out there. She's just hot from the car—the air-con isn't working.'

Jess smiled again, feeling her face tighten. She needed to tread carefully. 'As you have to see the doctor about the forms, you might as well get…' She tilted her head in enquiry.

'Moon.'

Jess tried not to skip a beat. 'Get Moon examined.'

'Well, I really don't have much time. She's breastfed, so she's getting antibodies. I don't think she needs to see a doctor.' Zondra's words came out bristly, as if she didn't really like being in this situation.

Jess chose not to tell Zondra that antibodies were highest before solid food was introduced. She didn't need to alienate her. 'Dr Fitzwilliam will be back—'

'I'm back.'

A tingle of longing zipped through her as Alex's deep voice sounded behind her.

He looked toward Zondra and Moon, a smile creasing his face. 'Is your little one not so well?'

Zondra snatched the papers out of Jess's hands and shoved them towards Alex. 'Actually, I just need you to sign some papers.'

Moon started to cry—a very high-pitched cry. Zondra jiggled her in her arms.

Alex looked at Jess, raising his brows in question.

Jess tried to send Alex some vibes to remind him

about her efforts to make links with the alternative community. Trying to keep her voice neutral, she spoke carefully. 'Ms Thompson requires the signature of a doctor on a school *immunisation* certificate stating her sons are not immunised.'

'I see.' He spoke the words slowly. 'Ms Thompson, are the boys with you?'

'No.'

'I'm sorry, but I can't sign this form without examining them.' Alex tried to hand the papers back to her.

'But they're not sick.' Zondra's voice started to rise.

'Your baby doesn't look well.' Alex's voice was neutral.

'It's just a cold. Look, I didn't come here for the third degree. I just need you to sign these forms. I don't want my kids immunised, and that's my right.'

'Is it?' A muscle twitched in his jaw.

Moon's cry became louder, more distressed.

Zondra moved the baby to her other hip, continuing to pat her on the back while she glared at Alex. 'Look, immunisation causes brain damage. I saw it on TV when I was pregnant with Shane.' Her defiant voice increased in volume to be heard over Moon's cry. 'No kid of mine is gonna become a vegetable.'

'So you'd prefer it if they died?' The words came out almost hollow.

A prickle of anxiety whipped through Jess. All colour had drained from Alex's face, and he gripped Zondra's papers so hard his knuckles gleamed white.

Such inflammatory words were *not* the way to handle Zondra. Jess couldn't let him alienate her. They needed an 'in' with the commune people.

She stroked the fretful baby's head. 'Zondra, the less people who are immunised, the greater the risk of an epidemic.'

The woman snorted. 'Epidemics are a thing of the past. That's a tired old argument you medical people trot out all the time. We're not living in Africa, you know.'

A sound like a growl startled Jess. She realised it had come from Alex's throat.

He slapped the papers down on the table and leaned forward, the muscles of his forearms bulging. 'Let me tell you something.' His voice came out deadly quiet, but laced with steel. 'Children die. They die from illness. They die from cancer and they die from preventable diseases because people like you don't immunise.'

Anguish seared his face for a brief moment, making Jess want to reach out and touch him. Give him comfort.

But then his eyes darkened to almost black and glittered with anger. 'Your ill-informed decision is not only putting your children at risk but others. When you decide to immunise your children, then I will sign your papers.'

'How dare you?' Zondra's face flushed puce. 'I've got my rights and I make decisions about my kids. You doctors are all the same.'

Stunned by Alex's over-the-top reaction, Jess struggled to think. She could see her chances of being welcomed as a health provider at the commune swirling quickly down the drain.

'Zondra—Doctor Fitzwilliam.' She tried desperately to infuse her voice with a conciliatory tone. 'I think we need to start over. I'm really worried about Moon, and I think as you're here Dr Fitzwilliam should examine her. Then later we can work through your concerns so you can see each other's point of view. Isn't that right, Alexander?' She looked pointedly at Alex, using his full name for effect.

He glared at her, his face stony.

'I'm not staying here a moment longer and I wouldn't trust *him* to look at my kids.' Zondra turned to leave.

Moon's cries stopped abruptly, and she started to shudder in her mother's arms.

CHAPTER FOUR

ZONDRA'S face paled with fear. 'What's happening?'

'Febrile convulsion.' Jess put her arms out and took Moon over to the examination couch. Laying the baby on her side, she quickly popped the buttons on the all-in-one to cool the baby down.

Alex swung his stethoscope up from around this shoulders, placing the earpieces in his ear, his total attention on the baby.

Jess put a thermometer in Moon's ear. It beeped. 'Forty-one degrees Celsius.'

Moon's body stopped twitching and she lay pale and still on the table.

'Will she be all right?' Zondra's voice was fraught with worry.

Alex pulled the stethoscope out of his ear. 'Children can fit when they have a high fever. We'll bring her temperature down and thoroughly examine her to see if there is more to this than just a viral fever.' He picked up the baby, cradling her gently, and passed her to her mother. 'She needs to be sitting upright on your lap when I examine her.'

Fear seemed to have pushed Zondra's antagonism

aside. She cradled the baby upright, Moon's back against her chest.

Moon leaned forward, her mouth open and her tongue hanging out. Her small chest retracted with the effort of trying to get air into her lungs.

'I need to listen to her breathing.' He gently placed the stethoscope on Moon's back. Concentration lines furrowed his brow.

He stood up and headed over to his medical bag. A muscle twitched in his jaw and the veins on his neck bulged as if he was struggling to rein in his anger.

Jess touched Alex's arm to get his attention. She spoke in a low voice. 'The baby was dribbling a lot when she arrived.'

He nodded. 'She's deteriorating in front of our eyes. Sudden onset of illness, high fever, dribbling, noisy breathing and not immunised. I can hear a soft stridor. I doubt it's croup. It'll be epiglottitis.' His hands clenched.

Jess's stomach lurched. Epiglottitis was a medical emergency, and they were out in the sticks. 'Will you have to intubate?'

His eyes flickered, his emotions at war. 'Pray we don't have to. I'm no paediatrician.'

His concern heightened her own. 'She'll need immediate hospitalisation. Ryeton hospital doesn't have a paediatric ICU. She'll have to go all the way to the Royal Children's Hospital in Melbourne.'

He nodded, his mouth a grim line. 'And quickly. Via the paediatric emergency transport service.'

'I better get hold of Phil to slash a helipad in the paddock next door.'

'Do that, and then get me the paediatric registrar from RCH on the phone.' He grabbed the portable oxygen cylinder, nebuliser and a paediatric mask, and strode back to his patient. 'Zondra, I'm going to need your help with this.'

Jess relaxed slightly as she punched numbers into the phone. He'd controlled his fury and frustration with Zondra, and his focus was now purely on helping Moon. But as soon as this emergency was over she was sitting Dr Alexander Fitzwilliam down for a very long talk.

He spoke quietly. 'Moon is having a great deal of trouble breathing. I'm going to give her some adrenaline through the nebuliser to help her. She has all the symptoms of epiglottitis, which means she has a blockage at the back of her throat that is preventing air getting into her lungs.'

The woman seemed to grip the baby closer to her. 'Oh, God—why?'

'Epiglottitis is caused by Haemophilus influenzae type B or HIB.' His voice sounded weary.

Zondra didn't lunge at him as before. 'Will she die?' Terror infused her whispered words.

'Not if I can help it.' With great tenderness he placed the mask on Moon's pale face and administered an adrenaline nebuliser. 'Is she allergic to penicillin?'

Zondra shook her head. 'I don't know. She's never had it. No one in the family has.'

'She needs it to fight the infection.' He seemed to almost drag in a breath, putting extra restraint on his anger. 'Zondra, this disease is highly contagious, and it's what the Health Department call a "notifiable disease".

We need a list of names of all the families Moon's been in contact with in the last thirty days. They all need to be on prophylactic antibiotics. I'm assuming many of your friends haven't immunised their kids either, so they're all at great risk.'

Jess handed the mobile to Alex. 'RCH paeds registrar for you.'

He accepted the phone and walked a couple of steps away.

Jess watched all the fight go out of Zondra as the reality of the situation sank in. She put a hand on the woman's shoulder, all the while watching Moon's colour. Her lips were a worrying blue, and she was visibly tiring from her exertions to breathe.

She drew up Cefotaxime—the antibiotic Moon desperately needed to fight the raging infection.

Alex rang off the phone and took one look at Moon. He listened to her air entry again. 'Jess, get out the paediatric intubation gear. I need an ET tube two sizes smaller than the usual.'

She knew from the gruffness in his voice that he was worried. She grabbed the tiny laryngoscope and snapped it open, checking the light globe. In an ideal world, Moon would be in an ICU with X-ray facilities and a ventilator.

She turned to find Alex had Moon on her back on the examination couch. She handed the scope to him.

He raised his eyes to lock with hers, as if he was looking for something, needing something.

Exactly what, she didn't know—but words bubbled up inside her, needing to be said. 'Moon's lucky you're here.'

His shoulders straightened. 'Hold her still for me, please.'

He carefully inserted the tiny silver scope into Moon's throat to find the vocal cords.

Jess's heart quickened with anxiety. It would be extremely difficult to visualise the cords due to the swelling of the epiglottitis. She held her breath as he passed the tube down and gently withdrew the laryngoscope.

'I'm in. Attach the air viva.'

She quickly attached it and then carefully taped the tube in place. The tape looked enormous on Moon's small cheek.

Zondra's sobs sounded behind them.

Jess left Alex bagging the baby, providing much-needed oxygen, and turned to Zondra. 'The helicopter will be here soon, and she'll be on her way to the Royal Children's.' She put her hand on the woman's shoulder. 'Who can I ring for you?'

Zondra's eyes flitted from Moon to Jess and back again, fear, anxiety and desperation all merging to slash her face with pain. 'Umm…Craig…the kids… I…ring Craig.' Her hands went to her face.

'Can you remember his number?' Jess put her hands on Zondra, trying to give support and calm her down enough to get the phone number.

Zondra scrabbled through her brightly coloured tote bag, pulling out an address book. 'It's there—under C.'

As Jess started to punch in the number she heard the whirring of the helicopter. She glanced at her watch; amazed it had come so quickly. But she'd been so busy time had passed much more quickly than she'd thought.

'Jess!' Alex called her over. 'I'll carry Moon. You manage the air viva.' They walked quickly out of the hall, with Zondra following.

The bright red helicopter steadied down onto Phil's newly mown circle, the downdraft of the rotors kicking up hay and dust.

Ducking down under the rotors, they ran to the helicopter and handed Moon over to the PETS team.

Jess hailed Zondra to run under and get onto the helicopter. She had to yell to be heard. 'I'll ring Craig and explain what has happened.'

The woman nodded, hesitated, and then hugged Jess. 'Thank you for everything.'

The doors closed and the helicopter took off. Jess turned to find Alex standing stock-still a couple of metres away, his eyes glued to the receding aircraft.

He shoved his hands in his pockets and fell into step beside her. 'And David told me to come to the country for a quiet life.' He raised his brows. 'That little girl is not out of the woods yet—and all because of her ignorant and stupid mother.'

Jess couldn't let that pass. 'She might be ignorant, but you're an educated professional.'

'So what's your point?' His jagged voice scratched hard as he pushed open the hall door.

Frustration surged inside her. 'My point is that you're supposed to be rational, to educate, not alienate.'

'She's risking her children's lives, and you want me to be rational?' He ran his hand through his hair in a gesture that tugged at her. 'Kids are dying in Africa because of the lack of basic medicine. Medicine Australians take for granted but don't value.'

'Well, we have to *teach* them to value it. Telling a patient about conditions in Africa doesn't work, because it's not their reality.'

'It's *my* reality.' The bitterness in his voice shocked her.

She thought about his episodes of erratic behaviour over the last few days. A seed of an idea formed. 'Alex, what happened in Africa?'

His body stiffened. His hands clenched and released. Tension bounced off rigid muscles. For the briefest of moments his eyes closed, as if trying to shut out the world.

Jess experienced a moment of pain under her ribs as she watched him. This had to be the key—the demon that tormented him and made him act out of character.

Suddenly her watch beeped. Loud, sharp, electronic noise that ricocheted off the bare walls.

'Five o'clock, Jess. You said you couldn't be late back to Roseport. You need to go.'

Jess hesitated, torn between her need to hear Alex's story and not wanting to be late for Woody. But she recognised the grief and pain on Alex's face. He had a look that was reminiscent of her own when Elly and Patrick died. 'I can stay longer.'

He folded his arms across his chest. 'No, you can't. You need to leave.' Alex's voice was firm, unrelenting.

Ignoring his body language, she pressed on. 'I think you need to talk about this.'

He raised one eyebrow. 'Oh, so you're a counsellor now, are you?' Sarcasm laced the words.

Ignoring his grief-driven barb, she spoke the words

that needed to be said. 'I think whatever happened in Africa is affecting your work, affecting how you deal with patients.'

His face hardened, the planes of his cheeks stark in relief as he seemed to suck in a breath. 'I just saved that baby's life. You're the practice nurse, Jess, not a medical standards assessor. Stick to caring for the people of Roseport.'

Trying to rise above the pain of his personal attack, she gave it one last try. *'You're* one of Roseport's people.'

'No, I'm not. And I never will be.' He hauled open the heavy door and shoved Jess's bag into her arms. 'Go now, or you'll be late.'

Jess stepped backwards out through the door, which closed in her face. Stunned, she walked to the car, blind to everything around her as her thoughts pummelled her.

She sat down heavily in the car seat, her heart pounding so hard she was certain all of Veriparipna could hear. She'd got so close to pulling down his protective walls and he'd fought like a wildcat to protect himself, using words instead of talons.

She'd bled a little at his words. And she'd bled for him. Africa had wounded him badly. That much she knew. Whatever he was trying to hold in behind those walls he'd built kept spilling over.

The handsome new doctor, who had turned her world on its head with his smile, was a tortured soul.

She'd been as direct as she could be and he'd still pushed her away. His comment about never belonging to Roseport worried her. Would he even be at work on Monday?

She sighed, wondering what to do. Contacting David to talk about her concerns wasn't an option. He was out of phone range. And David knew Alex better than she did.

She really didn't know him at all.

Her mind painted a picture of him—sun-bleached hair, broad shoulders, and the piercing emerald eyes that had stared so long at her own lips earlier in the day.

Her heartbeat picked up again and a wave of increasingly familiar heat washed over her. She wondered what it would be like to be held in those strong arms.

Her watch beeped again. *Woody*.

Hell, she shouldn't be daydreaming about Alex. She shoved the key into the lock and fired the ignition. Responsible mothers didn't daydream about men. Woody deserved her undivided attention. And she planned to give him that all weekend. She'd worry about Alex on Monday.

Alex stood on the beach, the salt-laden wind whipping his hair, battering his body. Nature unleashing its power, pounding him.

He welcomed it.

God, he'd been a jerk. First he'd flown off the handle at Zondra Thompson, and then he'd turned on Jess.

The gorgeous Jess. He added 'intuitive' to his Jess list. She'd pieced things together and come up with Africa.

And like a determined terrier she'd kept at him, nipping at his heels, pushing for an explanation. An explanation she deserved.

And what had he done? He'd hidden behind anger. Anger was so much easier than the truth. The truth meant sympathy. And what was the point in that? He'd endured enough sympathy two years ago and none of it had brought Nick back.

Anger kept sympathy at bay.

Jess's shocked expression, the flush that had spread across her cheeks, the way she'd bitten her bottom lip when he'd fired off his verbal salvos, stayed sharp in his mind. She had no idea how sexy she'd looked. Part of him had wanted to push her away and the other part of him had wanted to kiss her senseless.

He dragged in a breath. He couldn't go on like this. Being rude to patients was pointless. And he couldn't keep putting Jess through the fall-out of his emotional rollercoaster. Perhaps she was right. Perhaps he should talk about it.

Hell, everyone had been telling him he needed to talk about it. David, his parents, the therapist he'd seen once. Now Jess.

Shoving his hands deep into his pockets, he braced himself against the strong easterly wind and trudged back to his car. Jess needed an apology for his rudeness. He wondered if pizza and red wine would help his cause.

The sun set like a ball of fire falling into the sea, the last vestiges of orange light shimmering across the ocean. Alex drove along Shore Crest Road, searching for house numbers between the thick tea-tree hedges.

Finding Jess might be harder than the apology.

Who was he trying to kid? The apology would be the hardest thing he'd done in a long time. And the apology couldn't happen without an explanation. And that meant telling her everything. His throat constricted and he reached to loosen his tie. His fingers touched bare skin.

He shifted the gearstick into second and his car climbed the steep hill. The view of the southern ocean, with Roseport Bay nestling in front of it, spread out in front of him. He could see the Parkinsons' house in the distance, and the flashing beacon on the breakwater.

Thoughts tumbled through his head. *How to apologise without falling to pieces.* Sounded like a catchy self-help book title. He'd produce his peace offerings, get the apology over, and then take advantage of getting to know Jess away from the office.

He glanced at his watch. Nine p.m. What if she wasn't home? His stomach fell at the unwanted thought. Her sarcasm about a scorcher of a date had made him think that whatever she'd needed to leave for wasn't a date. And she'd left early. Even in the country, he doubted dates started at five-thirty.

He stopped the car at the top of the hill. Seventeen, Shore Crest Road. Alex peered up at the sleek and modern architecturally designed home, built into the cliff and rechecked the number written by Anna on the Post-it note. The numbers matched.

Jess lived *here*? Somehow he'd pictured her in a cottage or a renovated holiday shack, with windchimes and Buddhist prayer flags hung between the trees, and the occasional rustic crayfish pot.

He certainly hadn't pictured her in such a grand house. Not on a community health nurse's salary. He suddenly realised he knew very little about her apart from the fact she was a nurse. A very desirable nurse.

And he'd assumed from the absence of rings on her fingers she was single.

Hell, he should have asked Anna for details. Too late now. He was here and he had to go through with it.

He stepped out of the car, gravel crunching loudly under his feet, disturbing the cicadas' song. Juggling the pizza, flowers and red wine, he moved up the veranda steps and pushed the doorbell. He heard it chime in the distance.

Silence.

What if she wasn't home? He needed to get this apology over as soon as possible. Every muscle in his body tightened like an overwound clock.

The silver and grey door opened. Jess's eyes widened, surprise sparking in their velvet depths. 'Alex?'

His mentally rehearsed speech stalled as she stood in front of him. Her hair, which he had always seen tied back, was loose, cascading across her breasts, which were covered in a sleeveless, low-cut top.

He dragged his gaze away from the hint of rounded mounds of soft creamy skin. God, he was staring like a fourteen-year-old schoolboy.

Their words collided.

'Would you like to come in?'

'Can I come in?'

He adjusted the pizza box so the wine didn't crash to the ground.

Jess laughed, a tinkling sound that warmed him. 'Please, come in.'

'I come bearing peace offerings.' He held out the flowers.

She accepted the cornflowers. 'So I see.' She grinned at him. 'But you really only needed to bring chocolate.'

His heart-rate, already pounding, did a funny jump at her smile. 'Damn—does that mean negotiations can't commence?'

'I'll consider it over a glass of wine. Bring the pizza down to the kitchen.' She turned and walked towards the back of the house.

Alex stepped inside. Light and space surrounded him. Sleek modern lines and an open-plan design gave a sense of light and space. Cathedral ceilings and enormous full-length windows maximised the view of the ocean. The few walls which were not windows were decorated with modern art, including what appeared to be an original Pro Hart. A large spiral staircase wound its way to an imposing second storey. Thirty squares of luxury living and entertainment space.

His stomach sank. She didn't live alone. This house suited an entrepreneur more than a community health nurse. He stopped walking. He couldn't do this apology in front of someone else.

'Keep walking—you're nearly there.' Jess's voice called from behind an angled half-wall.

He realised he hadn't heard her talk to anyone else, or announce his arrival. Perhaps she was home alone. He pushed himself forward and around the corner.

'I thought you might have got lost.'

'No, I wasn't lost. Just admiring the artwork.'

She gave him a quick smile and opened a cupboard to grab some plates. As she stretched, her blouse rose up, exposing a flash of smooth skin.

The pizza and wine he held clattered onto the island bench. Air shuddered into his lungs. He righted the bottle of wine.

'You'll need this.' She opened a drawer and handed him a corkscrew.

Her fingers brushed his hand and a wave of electric shocks ricocheted through his body, leaving small fires of heat in their wake. 'Thanks.'

He concentrated on removing the cork from the Merlot and steadying his breathing, which marginally slowed his heart-rate. He was here to apologise. He needed to get that over, have a social chat, and leave.

He poured the wine, the glugging sound reverberating in his ears.

Jess placed the pizza on plates and picked them up. 'We'll picnic by the view. You bring the wine.'

She walked across the room, completely oblivious to the way her hips swayed, and the effect of the material of her shorts moving across her behind.

He gripped the stems of the wine glasses more firmly than he needed. Breathing deeply, he relaxed his grip.

Jess put the pizza on a large coffee table and then sat on the couch, tucking her feet underneath her. She looked like a teenager instead of a qualified nurse. For the first time he glimpsed some vulnerability and uncertainty in her face.

Alex handed her a glass of wine but remained standing. 'Great view.'

She raised her eyebrows. 'It is. But I'm certain you didn't come here just to admire it.'

He'd stalled enough. He took in a steadying breath.

'You're right. I came to apologise for this afternoon. You were correct. I was unprofessional and I shouldn't have vented my anger on Zondra Thompson. Or you.' God, he sounded so formal.

He could feel her searching gaze on his face, but she remained silent.

Her silence drove him on. 'Jess, I'm so sorry. You're a fantastic nurse, and of course you've got counselling skills. I deeply regret what I said to you.' He ignored the pounding sound in his head and the tightness in his chest. 'You're right. What happened in Africa *is* affecting my work.' He took a large drink of wine. 'And I probably should talk about it.'

She tilted her head slightly, encouraging him to start. 'I'm happy to listen if you think it will help.'

He didn't know if it would, but it was worth a shot. 'Three years ago I went to Ethiopia. I was on a personal mission to save the world.' He started to pace across the room; he had to keep moving.

'Penny, my wife, didn't want to go. She'd married a city doctor and she wanted the lifestyle that went with it. Roughing it in Africa was a long way from her long lunches in trendy South Yarra.' He sighed. 'But I convinced her to come. Our son, Nick, turned four when we arrived.'

He saw surprise register on her face at the mention of a son.

Nick.

A picture of Nick racing towards him, his arms outstretched, shot into his mind. The memory of his warm body snuggled in against his own winded him.

Jess's gentle voice brought him back to the present. 'Where were you based?'

'I divided my time between Addis Ababa and outreach to distant villages. Nick adored the villages. He picked up the dialects so quickly that he was teaching us. You see the world differently through the eyes of a child.'

He spun the stem of his wine glass through his fingers and focussed his gaze on the sparkling crystal. The faces of his African patients floated through his mind.

'You loved working there, didn't you?' Jess spoke softly.

He looked up and smiled at her, wondering at her constant perception. 'I did. Despite the political unrest, the famine and the drought, Ethiopia is a beautiful country. The people are amazing in their resilience.'

'Did Penny settle in?'

'No, she didn't. I loved everything about the place and she hated it. She wanted to go home. I persuaded her to try one more village rotation with me.'

'It must have been hard for you both.' Her voice vibrated with understanding.

Would she judge him harshly when she knew the full story?

He pushed on; there was no turning back. 'Things improved slightly, and I remember some good times in those last few weeks. Until Nick got sick.'

The tightness in his chest extended to his throat. His body felt as if it was encased in unrelenting steel.

Jess sat calm and still, patiently waiting for him to continue. Beautiful and serene, her gaze never left his face.

He needed to be near her. Her serenity and calming aura beckoned him. He moved across the room and sat down opposite her.

Against a constricted throat, he forced out the words he hated to speak. 'My beautiful, vibrant, inquisitive son got meningococcal serotype B meningitis and died two days later.'

'Oh, God, Alex…' Jess's voice cracked.

'*I* killed him.' He choked on the words and fought to breathe. 'I killed him because of my ridiculous dream to save lives. I sacrificed him to the greater good. And for what?' He pushed his head into his hands, pulling at his hair as Nick's pale face flashed through his mind, the image ripping at his heart.

Jess's voice pierced his shroud of anguish. 'You didn't kill him, Alex. Meningococcal killed him. *You* tried to save him.'

Bitterness welled up inside, scalding him. 'And a fat lot of good my medicine did. Penny reminded me of that often enough before she left.'

Suddenly Jess was off the couch, on her knees in front of him, her hands resting on his thighs. 'Alex, look at me.'

He raised his head and looked into her eyes, pools of liquid warmth drawing him in. Mesmerising.

'Nick could have died of meningitis in Australia. You know the odds. There's no vaccine for that strain yet, and even though you're a doctor you can't work miracles.' She gently placed her smooth palm on his stubble-roughened cheek. 'As much as we want to, we can't control everything in our lives.'

Her face reflected understanding and caring mixed in with sorrow. There was no sign of the uncomfortable and distant sympathy he was used to when people discovered he was a grieving father.

It had been such a long time since he'd opened up to anyone. Suddenly he wanted her comfort. He needed it. He leaned forward, dropping his head onto her shoulder, breathing in the scent of her hair, absorbing her vanilla perfume.

The tightness in his chest loosened. The bile in his throat receded. Calmness descended. He relaxed into her soothing embrace. A form of peace that had been missing in his life for so long settled over him. He soaked it up.

Jess's hands softly patted his back, then stroked his hair.

Calmness fled as her fingers caressed him, sending waves of heat thudding through him. Desire, hot and strong, flared inside him, licking at his grief, blazing for the first time in two years.

Was he confusing concern with something more? He lifted his head and hooked his gaze to hers, recognising the same spark of longing in her eyes. She felt it too. That heightened awareness that had been channelling between them since they'd met.

She held his gaze, swallowed hard, and then nibbled her plump bottom lip.

The action undid him. He groaned and gave in to the surging need. Cupping her face between his hands, he brought his lips gently down onto hers. She tasted of wine and honey, warmth and passion.

She leaned into him and welcomed him, opening her mouth to his, offering herself to him. Her tongue hesitantly stroked his lips, the tentative action stoking the flame of desire that burned so brightly inside him.

He'd been right. She wanted this kiss. He craved her touch, the sensations she sparked inside him. He pulled her close, needing to feel her against him, to have her heat flood him. To take what she offered.

He longed to feel more of her, taste more of her. He ran his tongue along her jaw, savouring her soft skin, pliant under his lips.

She arched against him with a muted groan and tilted her head back, her slender neck inviting his touch.

He dipped his head to trail kisses along her neck. Her hands gripped his hair and her mouth found his ear. Colours exploded in his head.

Driven forward by her urging, he slipped his hands under her blouse and his fingers discovered silken skin. Smooth and flawless.

He gently sat her down onto the couch. Her hands wound their way under his shirt, exploring his back, their feather-like touch bombarding him with pulsing waves of sensation until he thought he would explode.

Leaning back, she gently pulled him towards her.

He put his arm out to take his weight, but it slipped down the side of the couch. Something hard and sharp cut into his palm. 'Ouch! What on earth have you got down there?'

He dug down behind the cushion and pulled out a small toy truck.

Jess pushed against him and sat up, her face flushed.

Her eyes, glazed with desire, cleared instantly as she focussed on the toy truck. Anxiety lined her face. 'Sorry. It belongs to my nephew, Woody.'

Her anxious look confused him. He didn't want to think about it. Didn't want to know what it meant. All he wanted was her back in his arms. He wanted to feel her touch on him again, feel the way she drove his grief back down where it belonged, feel the passion in her kisses.

'Well, he'll be pleased we found it next time he visits.' He put the truck on the coffee table. Turning back to her, he drew her close.

Jess stiffened in his embrace and her luminous eyes filled with worry. A sigh shuddered through her.

He dropped his arms and pulled back, cursing the toy truck for breaking the moment.

'Alex...'

Her voice sent a chill along his spine. What was going on? 'Jess?'

She lifted her gaze to his, determination clearly marked on her face. 'Woody lives with me. My sister and brother-in-law died two months ago and I'm his guardian. He's my little boy.'

Her words, as powerful as gunshot, slammed into him. A child. She had a child.

Blood pounded in his ears, and cold sweat beaded his brow. Somehow he found his voice. 'How old is he?'

'Almost two.' She reached out to touch him, but he stood up abruptly and strode to the window.

She had a toddler. A little boy just a couple of years younger than Nick had been.

His throat constricted at the thought. His chest refused to expand. He had to get out of here.

He turned to find Jess just behind him. 'Alex, we can talk about this…'

'I have to go.' He pushed past her and strode down the passageway, out into the cool evening air.

Jess stood in the middle of the room, the amazing ocean view blurred behind tears of frustration and pain. Again, Alex had walked away from her. Only this time she knew why. And knowing didn't help.

She heard the car door slam, followed by the squeal of tyres as he pulled out of the driveway and drove down the hill. Her heart contracted in pain. She'd lost a dear sister and brother-in-law, and she ached for them. But to lose a child…

A tear splashed down her cheek, followed by a second and a third until she gave in to them. She cried for the loss of her sister, for Woody's loss of loving parents, and for Alex.

Finally, she dragged in a ragged breath and blew her nose. Time to tidy up and go to bed. Automatically she started plumping the flattened couch cushions, and immediately the memory of being in Alex's arms assaulted all her senses.

His scent of fresh air and sunshine, the feel of his taut muscles underneath tanned skin, his taste of salt and wine; it all came flooding back, threatening to drown her.

Her heart picked up its beat, her blood heating at the memory of being with him. When his arms had encased her, pulling her against him, she'd lost the battle with herself. She'd wanted his kiss. Craved it.

Three days of heightened awareness around each other had exploded. She'd come alive with his touch. Frissons of delicious sensation swirled through her just thinking about it. That she'd been swamped with such a driving desire stunned her. She'd never felt like that with any man. It made her feelings for Robert look chaste.

But the memory of Alex's tortured look when she'd told him about Woody sliced through the desire, grounding her rapidly.

She'd wanted to comfort him, hold him, but he'd rejected her. And in doing so had rejected Woody.

Robert had rejected her because she had a child. Now Alex. Did she seek out men who she knew wouldn't commit to her?

She gave herself a shake. Of course she didn't. She'd just for a brief moment let her loneliness and irrational desire interfere with her common sense.

She'd known all along that her gut instincts about Alex were right. Now she knew the reason he'd built walls around himself, holding himself distant. He was still grieving. And he wasn't remotely ready for a relationship, or to be a father again.

Now she knew the whole story she would be safe from letting her imagination run away with itself. Sure, he was handsome. Sure, he made her heart beat faster, made her day with a smile. But nothing could ever happen between them. The kiss was an aberration. A one-off experience.

She turned off the lights and walked upstairs.

Peeking in on Woody, she tucked a cotton blanket over him. 'Looks like it's just you and me, mate.'

Ignoring the growing empty space inside her, she went to bed.

CHAPTER FIVE

ALEX swore that the weekend had been longer than forty-eight hours. He'd spent a lot of Sunday sea-kayaking, pitting himself against the ocean. Finally, by the end of the weekend, with every muscle in his body rebelling with fatigue, he'd fallen into an exhausted sleep.

Sleep was becoming a problem. It either eluded him or was filled with technicolour dreams of Jess, which woke him with a start. Whichever way, he spent a lot of time staring at David's ceiling.

Come to Roseport. You can have a rest and find your love of medicine again. David's voice replayed over and over in his head.

He couldn't deny how much he enjoyed the challenge and the diversity of medicine that the Roseport practice was throwing at him. And he'd certainly dealt with some confronting emergencies.

The fall-out from the epiglottis incident was continuing as he grappled with the commune and the Health Department, organising the prophylactic antibiotic therapy. He'd even spent a large part of Saturday at the commune, working alone. Jess always had weekends off. Now he understood why. And why she needed to leave on time each day.

She was a mother.

An image of Jess's heart-shaped face and large brown eyes floated through his mind. He tried to shut it out.

Even harder was shutting out the memory of how he'd felt in her arms. But he wouldn't dwell on that. Jess had a child. He couldn't—wouldn't—love a child again; it hurt too much.

Besides, Jess was his colleague. And it was important to keep their work relationship straightforward, and not blur it with other personal issues.

Yeah, right. Who was he kidding? She was more than a colleague. The kiss they'd shared testified to that. So what fell in between colleague and lover?

Friend?

He ignored the flip of disappointment that swirled in his gut. Instead he moved his stare from the white paint of the ceiling and started counting the lines on the smoke detector above his bed.

'Anna, do I have any other patients before afternoon session?' Alex leaned against the reception desk, surprised at the empty waiting room.

Anna laughed. 'Sunny day, Doc. The tourists are at the beach and the locals are at Wednesday bingo.'

'But last Wednesday wasn't quiet.'

'That's because you were new. They were scoping you out.' Anna skated her office chair over to the filing cabinet.

Alex shook his head in wonder. 'The country ticks to a different clock, doesn't it?'

'Thank goodness it does.' Anna skated back. 'So why not take advantage of the lull and go for a surf? Or go out for lunch? I don't need you back here 'til two.'

Alex hesitated for a moment, unused to having free time in the middle of the day.

Anna gave him a knowing look. 'Jess just took her sandwiches over to the beach.'

'I *am* capable of spending lunchtime on my own, Anna.' Alex cringed at the unexpected supercilious tone in his voice.

''Course you are, Doc. But Jess has been looking drawn and tired. I'm sure she could so with some cheer-up company. And I'm stuck here manning the phones, so the job's yours.'

She threw him her 'off-you-go-then' look. He'd been organised and dispatched. How did receptionists manage that?

He shrugged in resignation. He hadn't seen much of Jess since he'd fled her house on Friday night. She'd been busy with her own clinics, and the few times they had been together work had filled the awkward void. Had Anna sensed the awkwardness? Was that why she was pushing him to join Jess?

He swallowed a sigh. It was looking as if lunch was the place to start his new friendship with Jess. The necessary platonic friendship. 'We'll be back at two.'

He pushed the clinic doors open and walked down the street to the milk bar. While he waited for his falafel and coffee he stared out of the window and across the road at Jess.

She sat at a picnic table, her head bowed, reading

the paper. The light breeze whipped strands of chestnut hair around her face and she absentmindedly tucked them back behind her ears. Her beige-coloured cargo pants seemed very tame compared with her usual jumble of colour. His gaze wandered lower and he laughed when he saw her bright red shoes. Colour spun off her like silk from a shuttle, weaving an intriguing magic.

A magic he had to forget. Friendship was their only option.

He paid for his lunch and walked across the road.

'Can I join you?'

Jess looked up, surprise and concern crossing her face. 'Of course you can. That would be great.' Her voice sounded strained. She closed the paper. 'How are you?'

He took the top off his coffee, the steam curling up into the already humid air. 'Better than I was last week. You were right. Talking about things did help.' He met her gaze. 'I'm sorry I raced off the other night, but I had no idea you had a child. The news was a bit of a shock.'

She gave a wry half-smile. 'It's still a shock and a surprise to me.' She fiddled with the edge of the paper. 'One minute I was living in Melbourne, Unit Nurse Manager at the George Hospital, and now I'm here, mother of Woody.' Her voice cracked and she bit her lip.

Her barely reined in grief swirled around him. He briefly touched her hand, his fingers skimming across her skin, absorbing her softness. 'You look tired.'

'I'm exhausted. Woody's still teething. I pulled him into bed with me last night. I used to think parents who had their kids in bed with them lacked discipline conviction. Funny how you'll trade all your best intentions for sleep.' Her laugh sounded strained.

A memory of walking the cold winter floors with a crying Nick surfaced. He wished he could lean forward and caress away the fatigue lines around her eyes. 'Broken sleep is a form of torture in some countries.'

'Now you tell me.' Her smile didn't quite reach her eyes.

'Don't you have family who can give you a hand?'

Jess shook her head. 'Mum and Dad are retired in Queensland, and although they can visit every couple of months they're not up to taking on raising a toddler. My brother-in-law was an only child, and his parents died a few years ago. So it's Woody and me.'

He heard sadness behind the false brightness in her voice. 'I'm guessing that amazing house belonged to your sister and her husband?'

She nodded. 'It does. Did.' She sighed. 'Right now Woody has enough to contend with, without adding moving into the equation, so I'm living there. It isn't really me. It's so enormous. We rattle around in it.'

A small pile of crumbled polystyrene gathered around her cup as her fingers worried the lip. 'Elly and Patrick regularly filled it with parties and people. I'd prefer a sandstone cottage, but right now I'm not making any big decisions.'

A glow of self-satisfaction spread through him. He'd *known* that modern glasshouse didn't suit her.

'Did they entertain for fun or business?'

'Both. They owned The Provedore in the main street,

and it's currently being managed with a view to sale. It's a thriving business, with gourmet food and the best coffee in town.' She raised her brows at his coffee cup. 'Real coffee, not muddy water.'

He grinned. 'Next time I promise I'll walk further for my coffee. Although Abra's coffee is a form of reminiscence. It reminds me of my intern days and hospital coffee.'

'Coffee you can stand your spoon up in? Some things are really best forgotten.' This time her smile lost its tightness and reached her eyes, sending out a shower of cheeky flares.

The now familiar warmth he experienced when he was with her spread through him. His body was betraying his head. He dragged his gaze from her face and concentrated on his lunch.

'The coffee's still good, even though Elly and Patrick don't make it any more.' Her smile faded.

'What happened?' He didn't want to add to her pain, but he had an intense need to know as much as he could about her situation.

'Patrick loved to fly, and he combined his passion with business. He regularly went to King Island to buy cheeses for the shop, or to wholesale to other businesses in the district. Elly normally stayed home, but this particular trip coincided with their wedding anniversary. So they had a weekend away together on the island. On their return journey the plane went down into Bass Strait, taking both of them with it.'

I'm sorry for your loss. The words sounded in his head and he went to speak them—but stopped himself.

He'd heard them often enough when Nick had died to know they didn't help. 'Hell, Jess, that really sucks.'

Her eyes widened as his words sank in. Then she tilted her head. 'You're right. It totally sucks. Life can change in a heartbeat.' Horror streaked across her face. 'Oh, God, I'm so sorry. You know that already.'

No! The word screamed in his head. He didn't want Jess tiptoeing around him like everyone else. He liked the straight-talking Jess. 'Don't apologise. I don't have a monopoly on sadness. You lost a loving sister and your life's been turned upside down. You're entitled to feel cheated.'

Suddenly her face hardened, her eyes sparking anger. 'I love Woody to death. I couldn't imagine my life without him.'

Her defiant voice spoke volumes. But he hadn't meant cheated out of life by becoming a mother. Normally Jess was easy-going, quick with a laugh. This was a new side to her. What had Jess given up to come here? Had she left someone behind in Melbourne?

Suddenly he was desperate to know that too. To know as much as he could about Jess. Friends knew that sort of thing about each other, didn't they? It wasn't outside the realms of friendship. 'Of course you love Woody. That goes without saying. But I doubt you saw yourself living the life of a sole parent.'

The fire of anger in her eyes faded. 'No, you're right. I had stars in my eyes. I thought I'd have a man by my side and we'd raise Woody together.' Her voice dropped. 'But I thought wrong. The moment he heard about Woody he bolted.'

Horror struck him deep in the solar plexus. Surely she didn't think their kiss had meant a commitment? 'Jess…about the other night—the kiss. I…'

Pink stained her cheeks. 'Not you.' Her hands fidgeted. 'Heavens, I'm not talking about *you*.' She laughed a brittle sound. 'We both know that kiss was just a one-off, brought on by an exhausting day of high emotion.' Her matter-of-fact tone was back.

He waited for relief to flood him at her interpretation of the kiss.

'No, I was talking about Robert Blinkerman, Cardiologist. Man about town and total…' Her voice trailed away.

'Bastard?' He filled in the blank.

She smiled. 'Exactly. Total bastard. Do you know him?'

He tried hard to ignore the spinning sensation in his gut created by her smile. 'Not really. I've referred a few patients to him. How long were you together?'

'Three years.' Her words sliced the air, jagged and sharp.

'Ah. Long enough to expect a commitment?'

She nodded and sucked in her bottom lip, her teeth grazing it.

Her involuntary reaction triggered the memory of her teeth grazing his ear. White heat shot to his groin. He found he was gripping his lunch a little too hard, and tabouli juice and garlic sauce ran down his wrist.

'Exactly. Seems I was a bit slow working him out.'

Her self-deprecating humour made him smile. She radiated an inner strength that amazed him. Her life had been turned upside down, but she mostly faced it head on.

'Looking back, I ignored a lot of signs. It appears we had totally different expectations of the relationship. I thought we were both there for the long haul. He thought I was handy to have around. Until I came with a child.' She grimaced and then shook her head, as if shaking off the past.

'So now I'm here in this gorgeous place, with my little boy.' She moved her arm in an arc to encompass the view. 'And Robert can keep his big city, his cocktail parties, his Wednesday game of golf, and stick it up his jumper.'

He raised his coffee cup. 'Good for you.' But he could see the hurt reflecting back at him from the depths of her chocolate-brown eyes. She'd lost more than her sister. She'd lost her dream.

She tilted her head and gave him a long look, which suddenly turned into a cheeky grin. 'So, now you know the whole story. You can relax around me. You're safe. The kiss happened and it's over. I have no intention of marching you or anyone else down the aisle.'

'Yeah, well, I'm with you there. My own trip down the aisle wasn't rivetingly successful. Penny and I were mismatched from the start. Even if Nick hadn't died, our marriage was already struggling badly.' He heard the words come out of his mouth, surprised he'd voiced them. He'd never told anyone that before.

'Sorry.'

'Don't be.'

For a moment Jess was silent, staring out towards the horizon. Her long dark lashes stroked her cheeks when she blinked.

His heart pounded in his chest. This strong and gorgeous woman deserved a man to love her and her son. But he couldn't offer her that.

And she didn't want it. She'd put Woody's needs ahead of hers before she'd ever risk her heart again.

That thought alone should relax him.

She turned back. 'You're here for three months, Alex. I hope you can consider me a friend.'

He saw trust, respect and understanding on her beautiful face. He searched for signs of the passion she'd shown in his arms. He saw none.

She wanted to be his friend. Nothing more. He had what he wanted.

The relief he'd expected didn't come.

'Two boxes of syringes,' Anna called out from behind a pile of boxes.

'Check.' Jess ticked the inventory form. She was glad of the menial, routine stock-take of the treatment room because she couldn't concentrate on much else. Her thoughts were full of Alex.

They were now officially friends. After three days of existing in a maelstrom of emotion, friendship didn't seem quite enough. But what choice did she have?

The look of horror on his face when he'd thought she wanted a relationship with him had sealed what she already knew.

Alex didn't want another relationship. Especially one where a child was involved. And she wouldn't risk Woody. He deserved a man who would love him like a father.

The disappointment that had swirled inside her at his expression of dread still confused her.

She had thought she was fine with both of them not wanting a relationship. She would just go to work, do her job and go home again. But at lunch Alex had listened to her, drawn her out, and he was the first person who seemed to truly understand how she felt about her new life.

She wanted that understanding. She wanted to feel connected to Alex in some way other than just as a colleague. He was only in town a short time, so the solution seemed to lie in their being friends. So she'd offered him friendship.

So how did a *friend*, who longed to have her *friend's* arms around her, act? How did she hide the shimmering longings for his touch? The cravings to feel his skin against hers?

A friend should stick to spending time with him at work only. Yes, that was the solution.

'Come in, Jess!' Anna's voice broke through her thoughts.

'Sorry?'

'Normal saline one-litre IV's—one box. You're a bit distracted.' Anna moved off the stepladder. 'By the way, did Dr Fitzwilliam find you at lunchtime?'

Jess caught Anna's coy look. 'Yes, he found me at the beach. Did you draw him a map?'

'Oh, come on, Jess. Lighten up. You have to admit he's easy on the eyes. Plus, he's a lot more settled this week. No more Dr Grumpy.'

'True, but he's recovering from some pretty heavy

personal stuff, so any notions you have of pairing me up with him stop right now. OK?'

Anna's face paled. 'I had no idea. Anything I should know about? I would have thought David might have mentioned something.'

She shrugged. 'I guess it's Alex's information to tell. Plus, David raced off so fast we were lucky he even told us Alex was coming.' She smiled fondly, recalling David's dynamo approach, which never left time for the small details.

'Do you think he's up to attending the grass tennis tournament?' Anna suddenly looked anxious. 'David was supposed to present the prizes and play. The Ladies' Auxiliary will be really upset if a doctor isn't involved, and you know how generous they are with their fundraising. David wouldn't have been able to get the defibrillator at the lifesaving club without their contributions.'

'I have no idea if he'll do it. Ask him.' Jess turned over the stock-take form.

'Could you ask Alex? Please, Jess.'

'Ask me what?'

Surprise and pleasure zipped through Jess on hearing his voice. She turned to face him. 'You've been dobbed in to be the "cause célèbre" at the Friends of Medflight Lawn Tennis Round Robin.'

'Really?' He grinned a full-dimpled smile. 'Can I say no?'

'Absolutely not. David would never forgive you.' She hoped her brisk voice covered the fact that her knees had turned to jelly with one glimpse of his smile.

'You have to take a partner, Doc. It's a doubles tournament.' Anna swooped her arm back behind her, pretending to play air-tennis.

'Would *you* like to partner me, Anna?'

Anna paused mid-air-serve. 'Oh, that's sweet, Doc, but I can't actually play. Jess, however, is a wicked player.' Anna threw her a sly look.

Panic flooded every part of her. Just the thought of Alex in tennis whites brought her out in a sweat of pure lust. She quickly protested. 'It's on a Saturday, and Woody and I spend Saturdays together.'

'I'll mind Woody for the afternoon. He loves it at my place, and my kids adore having him around. Tenika will mother him to death.' She raised her brows. 'Besides, David would never forgive you if you didn't go.'

She pulled her jaw off the floor. She couldn't believe Anna had just dumped her into the tournament with Alex, minutes after she'd told her to back off. There was no way out. She'd used the same guilt line on Alex to force his hand. Now she was well and truly landed in it.

The blast of a car horn made her jump. Slamming doors quickly followed it.

'I need a doctor!' A frantic voice had them all running to Reception.

An agitated and dishevelled young man stood wringing his hands.

'What's the problem, mate?' Alex strode forward, his voice calm.

'My girlfriend's having a baby in the car. We tried to get to Ryeton but she wants to push, and—'

'I'll grab a delivery set and meet you out there.' Jess snatched a packet of gloves from behind the reception desk and shoved them at Alex. 'Anna, call an ambulance.' She quickly raced to the treatment room.

Hastily pulling a sterilised delivery set from the shelf, she also grabbed a couple of plastic aprons. A moment later she was in the car park. Alex's taut bottom was protruding out of the back door of a car.

He suddenly stood up, bumping his head hard on the doorway. He grimaced and rubbed his head.

'Any chance of her making it to Ryeton?' A niggle of doubt forced the words out of her mouth. A hospital delivery was always preferable. And it was over two years since Alex would have attended a birth. Would he cope emotionally with delivering a baby?

He raised his brows at her expression. 'Not a snowball's chance. She wants to push and she's fully dilated.' He closed the slight gap between them and gently squeezed her arm. 'I'll be fine.' He spoke quietly. 'And you're here, with your midwifery skills, so together we'll deliver this baby.'

His voice, velvet-soft, seemed to caress her. She wanted to lean into him and lay her head on his shoulder.

Forcing her attention away from Alex and onto their patient, Jess stepped back. 'Here—wear this.' She threw the apron over his head.

'Jess, you do the delivery and I'll receive the baby.'

Amazement and surprise collided inside her. She studied him closely. 'Are you sure?' Doctors usually couldn't keep their hands off a delivery.

He nodded. 'You've done this a bit more recently than me, so it makes sense. But I'm right beside you if you need me. We're a team.' He gave her a quick grin.

Dragging her gaze away from his dimpled cheeks, she turned to face the young man. 'I'm Jess. Now, you need to go around the car and support your partner. She might want to lean up on you.'

He nodded. 'I'm Tom, and Melissa's having the baby.' He ran around the car, opened the door and got into the back seat with Melissa.

Jess pulled on a pair of gloves and crawled into the car. 'Hi, Melissa. I'm Jess, I'm a midwife, and you've met Dr Fitzwilliam. Together, with your help, we're going to deliver this baby.'

Melissa nodded, biting her lip. 'Need to push—'

'Right—with the next contraction you can push. But while we're waiting I'll just put this plastic sheet under your bottom, to protect the car seat.'

'Bit late for that.' Tom's tone sounded resigned. 'Her waters broke about ten minutes ago. The upholstery is never going to be the same again.'

'Arrgh!' Melissa let out a groan and started to push, leaning back against Tom.

Jess gently placed her hand on Melissa's thighs so she could see what was happening. Sure enough there was a circle of black hair, crowning on the perineum. When the contraction stopped the baby's head didn't slip very far back.

'Great job, Melissa. With the next contraction I need you to push, but then stop pushing when I say. I want to guide your baby's head out slowly—OK?'

'I'll try, but it bloody hurts.' Melissa gripped Tom's hand. 'Got—to—push.'

'Here's the scissors and clamps.' Alex's arm manoeuvred around her to put a kidney dish down in front of Jess.

'Thanks.' She was struck by the oddness of this role reversal. She placed her forefingers on Melissa's perineum and gently kept the baby's head flexed, so the smallest diameter could slide through, hopefully avoiding a tear.

'Stop pushing, Melissa. Breathe the baby out.'

Melissa's panting gasps meant only the uterus was pushing. A gush of clear fluid hit the apron, and then the baby's head popped out.

'Well done, Melissa. I'm just checking the cord.' Jess inserted a gloved finger to feel for the cord. She could feel a loop of cord around the baby's neck. Gently, she tried to ease it over the baby's head, but it was wound around too tightly.

'Don't push, Melissa.' Jess quickly picked up the clamps, then carefully located the cord again and attached them.

'Everything all right?' Alex leaned in closely over her shoulder, his breath on her neck.

'Cord.' Jess's concentration was zeroed in on carefully cutting the cord without cutting either mother or baby.

'Anna, go and grab the portable oxygen.' Alex issued the brisk instruction.

The scissors lay heavy on Jess's hand as she quickly sliced through the now clamped but ill-positioned cord. She wound the cord and clamps out of the way so they hung down by the baby's head.

'Well done.' Praise sounded in Alex's voice.

'Arrgh!' The next contraction hit Melissa.

Gently guiding the baby's head downward, Jess delivered the top shoulder and then lifted the baby slightly so the bottom shoulder slithered out.

'Congratulations—you've got a beautiful baby girl.' Jess positioned the baby on her mother's stomach with the baby's head lying downwards to drain any secretions.

Melissa gingerly put her hand onto her daughter. 'Oh, Tom.' Melissa tilted her head back. 'Isn't she beautiful?'

Tom remained silent, struck dumb by the rapidity of events. But a wide grin split his face.

Jess moved sideways to create some more room in the cramped car, her back slamming into the front seat. She swallowed the 'ouch' she desperately wanted to voice.

Alex quickly leaned forward and gently placed a towel over the baby, drying her so she didn't get cold.

The baby lay limply, her colour a mottled purple. She didn't make a sound.

'The cord was around her neck pretty tight.'

Jess heard the anxiety in her own voice. Everything had happened so quickly, and there hadn't been time to take a foetal heartbeat. Who knew how long the baby might have been distressed?

Alex turned the baby over on Melissa's stomach and continued to rub her. 'Come on, little one. Start breathing.' His low voice, although calm, held a slight edge. He started to blow gently on her face, puffs of air, to kickstart the breathing response.

'Why isn't she breathing?' Melissa's voice started to rise in panic.

Jess passed Alex the meconium aspirator to clear the nose of any mucous. 'The amniotic fluid was clear.'

'Babies can do this sometimes, and this one's had a rush trip into the world.' Alex quickly squeezed the bulb of the aspirator, sucking any secretions from the baby's nose and mouth.

Jess assessed the baby's colour, breathing, heart-rate, reflexes and muscle tone. 'Apgar at one minute is three.' She bit her lip; ideally it should be eight to ten.

Jess heard Anna's pounding feet and reached out for the paediatric mask and Penlon bag. 'Turn the oxygen on full, Anna.' She gently placed the tiny mask over the baby's face and started to puff life-saving oxygen into the baby's unresponsive lungs.

Alex continued to rub the baby and tickle her feet, trying to stimulate her to start breathing.

Agitated silence pressed in on Jess. Melissa and Tom's elation plunged downward into fear. Jess sent up a quick prayer.

Suddenly a feeble whimper broke into the eerie silence, followed by a lusty cry. The baby's face creased in displeasure as it announced its true arrival into the world.

'That's my girl.' Alex turned the baby around so her face was up near her mother's.

Melissa clutched her daughter to her breast, tears welling in her eyes. 'Oh, thank you so much—both of you.'

'Yeah, thanks, Doc—Jess. Hell, I'm glad I knew where this clinic was.' Tom's heartfelt thanks, intermingled with relief, settled gently over Jess.

She smiled back. 'You're very welcome. It's always special to deliver a baby.'

'In fact, we should probably be thanking *you*.' Alex spoke quietly. 'It's been a long time since I had the privilege of attending a birth.'

A siren wailed and an ambulance pulled into the car park.

Jess started to clamber out of the car, her body grazing Alex's. Tingling sensations whizzed through her. Her coordination fled, clumsiness raced in.

Alex flattened himself against the back seat to make more room, but Jess tumbled over his feet, falling against him.

Shooting her hand out to steady herself, her palm connected with his shirt. Hard muscle and heat. She moved her head up and her eyes locked with his. Bright green and dark green swirled together, pulling her in.

Panic and passion collided.

She shot backwards and virtually fell out of the car at the ambulance officer's feet, her skirt tangled up around her waist.

'That's a good look, Jess.' Mick Hennessy reached down to pull her to her feet, grinning.

Trying to muster as much dignity as she could, she accepted his hand, straightened her skirt and tried to block out Robert's patronising voice. *Some decorum would be nice, Jess.*

The next moment Alex was standing by her side, his arm looped casually around her shoulder, giving her a quick squeeze. 'She's just done a fantastic delivery, guys. Shame you missed it.'

'Poaching the fun stuff again?' Mick grumbled good-naturedly.

'Always.' Alex's eyes twinkled. 'Jess will hand over while I check on mother and baby.' Alex climbed back into the car.

The heat from his hand lingered. Her heart-rate pounded off the scale. And Mick Hennessy's grin got wider. She mustered every ounce of professionalism she had. 'Melissa is a primigravida who had a precipitate labour and delivered a live baby girl at fifteen-twenty-five today.'

Five minutes later, handover complete, Jess turned to see Alex tenderly cradling the baby against his broad chest while the ambulance officers organised for Melissa to be loaded onto the rig. Something lurched deep inside her.

In the past week she'd seen him barricade himself behind protective walls, seen him as the brisk doctor-in-charge to cover his own pain, and she'd held him stricken with grief.

But right now she saw the wonder of the miracle of new life reflected deeply in his emerald eyes. And she suddenly saw how important being a father had been to him. How it must have defined him.

Pain, sharp and fresh, lanced her at his loss. His loss of Nick, and the loss of a lifestyle he'd once coveted. A lifestyle he now rejected.

Your loss too. The thought slammed into her, scaring her. She didn't want to think about Alex as a father. That was just too hard. Knowing he'd turned his back on family life. Knowing she had a little boy who needed a dad.

She must only think about Alex as a friend.

She banished the insistent voice.

Dragging in a breath, she walked over to him, fighting the strengthening desire to touch his arm, feel his warm skin on her own. She touched the baby instead.

'She's pretty cute.' Jess ran her hand over her head and tucked the bunny rug securely around her.

He looked up and smiled a lopsided grin. 'She'll be the apple of her father's eye.'

Jess looked away towards Tom, deliberately breaking Alex's gaze. Breaking away from the overwhelming desire to sink into eyes that were the colour of the Pacific.

She knew at that precise moment she'd seriously miscalculated her lunchtime offer. Being Alex's friend would be the hardest thing she'd ever done.

CHAPTER SIX

Water bottle, sunscreen, cap, muesli bar for energy, racquet, dress for the cocktail party... Jess ran through her mental list of all the things she needed for the tennis tournament. Alex was due to pick her up in fifteen minutes.

He'd been insistent that he would pick her up. She would have been happier to meet him at the courts, having first settled Woody with Anna.

She looked at her watch. Anna and Tenika should have been here already. They planned to take Woody to the beach and collect him on their drive over. After the beach he was going to have a sleepover at Anna's. He loved the beach and he adored Tenika. So he'd be having a great time while she faced an afternoon and evening of being with Alex with no work to put any distance between them.

Agitation bounced around her body; her stomach did flip-flops, her heart kept racing with runs of rapid-fire beats.

'Jess.' Woody, holding his spade with one hand and pulling her hand impatiently with the other, interrupted her thoughts. 'Dig in sandpit—now.'

'OK, mate. You've been patient. Let's go to the sandpit.' She could wait for everyone outside just as easily. But she hoped Anna would arrive before Alex.

Jamming her hat on her head, she let herself be instructed by Woody and sat down in the sandpit.

Squatting down next to her on his chubby legs, he pushed the bucket towards her. 'Make sandcastles, please.'

An exalted thrill tripped through her at his 'please'. For the last couple of weeks she'd been concentrating on Woody saying please and thank you. For the first time she really felt like a mother, proud of her child's achievements.

She started filling the bucket with sand then turned it over and patted the base with the spade. 'Abracadabra!' She lifted the bucket and exposed the sandcastle.

Woody gave a whoop of delight, and then jumped on the sand castle. 'All gone! 'Nother one—make 'nother one. Please.'

Jess laughed and refilled the bucket. If only she could stay here all day. The sandpit was a lot safer than the tennis tournament.

'Sorry we're late, Jess.' Anna raced breathlessly through the back gate and Tenika followed.

'Neeka!' Woody abandoned the sandpit and threw himself at the twelve-year-old girl, excitement lining his round face.

'I can see he's really going to miss me.' Jess looked over as Woody led Tenika behind the hedge and over to the swing set.

'You get ready. Woody will be fine with us. Go and enjoy yourself.' Anna walked over to join the children.

'Hello?' Alex's voice came down the drive.

Jess's stomach lurched and she scrambled to her feet as Alex walked through the gated archway.

The light emphasised the blond streaks in his hair. Dark sunglasses hid his eyes, but their vibrant green was imprinted on Jess's memory.

His mostly white polo shirt moulded to his chest and outlined his broad shoulders and firm biceps. He hadn't gone for the baggy shorts look. Tan skin and muscles which rippled with sinew were exposed from mid-thigh. Golden hair lined his athletic legs all the way to his ankles, and his feet firmly controlled the ground in a pair of state-of-the-art runners.

She didn't need her two a.m. fantasies; she had the real thing in front of her. She reminded herself to breathe.

He smiled. 'I rang the bell, but then I heard you outside so followed the sound.'

'Sorry. Anna was late, and I've been keeping Woody entertained.'

Shrieks of laughter came from behind the hedge as the swing rose up in the air.

Alex's head snapped around at the sound, his expression guarded behind his sunglasses.

Jess's heart seemed to stall. Up until now she'd made sure Alex hadn't met her little redheaded boy, whose colouring was so similar to his. She didn't think either one of them was up for a meeting.

She certainly wasn't up for it.

He smiled and turned back towards her. 'Sounds like they're having fun.'

Pushing the rising panic back down, she found

herself speaking rapidly in an overly bright voice. 'I need to say goodbye to him, so I'll just be a minute.' She started to walk away.

'Aren't you going to introduce me?'

His words hit, immobilising her. She didn't want to introduce him. She didn't want to complicate things any more than they already were. Her feelings for Alex were out of control as it was. Keeping him out of her 'at home life' with Woody was all she had left to hold onto.

She had to keep Woody safe. Woody had lost enough. He didn't need to bond with someone who would be gone in a few weeks.

But it isn't just Woody you're worried about. The voice in her head pounded out unwanted thoughts.

She pasted on a false smile. 'He's pretty settled with Tenika and Anna at the moment. I'd hate to interrupt them.'

Alex lifted his shoulders in a resigned shrug, his smile fading. 'Right, well, I'll meet you out in the car so you can disengage from Woody with a minimum of fuss.' His tone sounded hurt.

As he turned to leave, Woody suddenly ran back to Jess, his arms circling her knees. Her stomach plummeted. Panic overtook her. She had no choice. She had to introduce them.

Leaning down, she picked up Woody, cradling him against her hip. 'Woody, this is Dr Alex, who I've been working with while Dr David is away.'

Alex smiled, but she saw the tremor of tension across his high cheekbones.

He bent his knees slightly, so he was at the same eye

level as the little boy. 'G'day, mate. Were you having fun on the swing with Tenika?'

Woody squirmed in her arms, nodding. 'Push swing?'

Alex glanced at his watch.

Her heart thudded hard and fast. She didn't want him to push the swing. Didn't want him doing what he thought he should do out of politeness.

'Sure, I can push—'

She cut him off. 'Really, we have to go, Alex. The Ladies' Auxiliary will be really cross if you're late for your opening speech.' It sounded lame even to her ears, but she had an overwhelming need to separate the two of them.

Alex stood up. Surprise and hurt reflected back at her in those deep green eyes. 'Sorry, mate. Jess and I have to go—but Tenika will give you a swing.'

Prickles of unease jabbed her. Had she done the right thing? She breathed deeply. Yes, she had. She had the right to protect her child. That was her job. In fact, she was protecting Woody *and* Alex. Alex just couldn't see that.

Admit it. You're protecting yourself.

She and Alex had no future together; they both knew that, so why did he sound so hurt? And why did she care so much that she had been the cause?

Thwack. The tennis ball bounced off Alex's racquet and powered across the net. He was warming up and working off his frustration on the new fluoro green tennis balls.

He could see Jess, his partner for the day, out of the corner of his eye on the forehand side of the court. He knew Jess the nurse pretty well now, and he'd seen intriguing glimpses of Jess the woman, but an hour ago he'd come face-to-face with Jess the mother.

He'd had enough time to come to terms with the fact that Jess was a mother, but today he'd seen her in action, in full protective mother-hen role. And he'd been the big bad wolf. She hadn't wanted to introduce him, and when she'd been forced to she'd bustled him off so fast he'd barely been able to say hello. What did she think he was going to do to the child?

'Hey, Alex, save some of those shots for the actual game.' Mick Hennessy dodged a powerful volley.

'Right, mate. Sorry.' He hit the next ball more softly.

Jess had sat opposite him at lunch three days ago and offered him her friendship. If she'd said 'we can only be colleagues' he would have understood her reaction with Woody, but friends implied more than just talking at work. Friends meant spending time together out of work. And meeting her child.

Funny, he'd *wanted* to meet Woody. He hadn't thought he would, but the little boy was part of who Jess was, and he increasingly wanted to know Jess.

He didn't want to be an important part of the kid's life. He didn't really want any significant involvement. But he resented being totally banned from it.

He ran and scooped up a low ball with a sharp backhand cross-court shot, getting satisfaction from the way the ball dropped short on the other side.

His anger fizzled out.

Perhaps she was protecting you. The thought popped into his head. He'd been so taken aback about being rushed away from Woody that he hadn't thought of it from that angle. He'd been such a basket case when he'd first arrived. But recently Roseport did seem to be a balm to his soul, just like David suggested. He'd been far more relaxed this week—more than he had in a long time. More relaxed since he'd told Jess all about Nick.

Jess is the balm. The self-righteous voice that annoyed him at four in the morning spoke softly. He tried to ignore it. David was right. A change of lifestyle and more challenging medicine had done the trick. It would have happened even if Jess hadn't been in town.

'Damn.'

He turned to see Jess walking towards the fence to collect the ball she'd missed.

She'd pulled her gleaming hair back in a utilitarian ponytail and jammed a cap on her head. Yet there was nothing plain or no-frills about her. Her short white pleated skirt swirled around her toned thighs and her apple-green jersey top clung like a second skin, outlining her small, pert breasts.

His groin tightened. Hell, he had to play doubles with her all afternoon. And every time he looked at her he wanted to haul her into his arms, feel her softness against him and drink her in.

But friends didn't do that.

And each day it got harder to remember that.

Thank God for the physical release of tennis. He'd play out his frustrations against his opponents.

'Ready?' Jess, who had been very quiet since they'd left her house, walked over and smiled straight at him.

His blood turned into liquid heat. 'Ready.' His voice rasped out the word.

They won the toss and elected to serve. Jess took the balls from his hand, her fingers barely grazing his palm. But her slight touch generated such thundering sensations of longing he was thankful they were on a tennis court surrounded by people. Anywhere else, and on their own, he would have kissed her senseless and hoped for more.

Jess prepared to serve. She raised her racquet and a band of creamy skin appeared as she shot the ball into the opposition's service square.

His mind still clouded by the rise of Jess's shirt, he missed the fast ball Mick returned straight down his tramlines.

'Best to keep your eye on the ball, mate.' Mick grinned knowingly.

Hell, was it that obvious? Was he staring like a hormonal fourteen-year-old? He straightened his shoulders. Mind on the game, not on Jess. 'Beginners' luck, Mick. Don't get too cocky.'

Jess served again, and this time he was right in the action, volleying the ball back fast and hard. Mick and his partner, Jenny, played hard too, and an hour later they faced a tiebreak.

'Wow, this is really turning into a game.' Jess laughed, panting slightly as they changed ends. Exertion had flushed her face pink, and her eyes gleamed like melted chocolate. She tilted her head back and raised her water bottle to her rosy lips.

Like a rabbit caught in headlights, his gaze shot to her mouth. The memory of his lips against hers blasted through him like the heat from a raging furnace. His heart-rate pitched into overdrive—and he couldn't blame the exercise.

He fiddled with the strings of his racquet. 'If we keep playing like this we'll end up in the finals. You're playing incredibly—running every ball down.'

A shy smile crossed her face. 'Thanks. Although I doubt I'll be able to move tomorrow. I'm using muscles that haven't seen the light of day in a long time.'

She laughed and stretched her thigh by pulling her leg up behind her. 'I've only just got back into tennis, and we're so lucky here. Who in Melbourne can afford to play on grass courts? Plus the tennis club is a good place to meet people when you're new in town.' She waved to a young guy who hailed her as he walked past.

A streak of jealousy ripped through Alex. *He* wanted her wave and smiles. He wanted them to himself.

'Come on, then, we better get back to it.' He put his hand on the small of her back and guided her through the narrow gap between courts, the need to touch her too great to resist.

Alex walked down to baseline, preparing to serve the first ball of the tiebreak.

Jess stood up at the net, her back to him, her hips swaying in anticipation of the return of serve.

He groaned. He had to serve the ball past her, and she had no idea what a delightful distraction she was. Using every technique he knew to block out his surroundings, to block out Jess, he blasted the ball at Mick.

Jess blocked Mick's return with a deep volley, straight between Mick and Jenny, the chalk flying as the ball hit the baseline.

Her stellar play continued until the score was 6-5 in the tiebreak. If they won this point the match was theirs.

It was Alex's turn to serve again. Gripping the racquet, he threw the ball high in the air and brought it down hard, slicing the ball. It shot across the net and landed fast and hard in the backhand corner of the service square. An ace!

Jess gave a whoop of joy and ran back towards him. 'Fantastic shot!'

Instinctively he opened his arms to her.

She ran into them, jumping up and down, her enthusiasm infectious. 'I can't believe we won.'

He grinned at her delight. 'We did. What a team.' His arms closed around her, pulling her close, feeling her heart hammering against his chest, breathing in her vanilla scent, savouring the tickling sensation of her hair brushing his neck, and experiencing the thrill of holding her again.

Her laughter enveloped him and her touch sparked something inside him—a sense of exhilaration, of being alive. A feeling that had eluded him for so long.

She looked up at him, her eyes wide and round, her pupils black discs in a sea of brown velvet. And she smiled. An intimate, shared-secret smile.

His world tilted on its axis. Time stalled.

Suddenly she dropped her gaze and stepped back. His arms yielded to her pressure and fell away down by his sides. Air rushed in where she'd rested against him. Cold. Crisp.

The kernel of exhilaration shrivelled.

'We better go and shake hands with Mick and Jenny.' She turned and walked towards the net.

He watched her go. He wanted her back in his arms again. He wanted to feel that same intoxicating exhilaration. He sighed. Friendship with Jess wouldn't give that to him. He'd known it for a week, but it had just been rammed home loud and clear. He'd been a fool to think it would be enough.

But he wasn't heading down the road of another relationship. Matrimony didn't suit him. The only good thing to come from his marriage to Penny had been Nick. And he'd lost him.

But when Jess was in his arms life was bearable, and he wanted that feeling.

So where the hell did that leave him?

Jess blow-dried her hair in the tennis club's changing room, moving off to the side as far as the electrical cord would allow. It was just like school camp as women jostled for mirror space, lent each other make-up and generally acted like excited teenagers. With the tennis now finished, everyone was getting ready for the cocktail party.

Jess couldn't remember the last time she'd had so much fun. Spending a social day with grown-ups and not a toddler was a special treat. But even before Elly and Patrick's death fun hadn't been high on her agenda.

Robert's idea of a social outing had been dinner at a stuffy and overly expensive restaurant, or a dinner party for six at home, where the talk had droned on about hospital politics. She'd usually ended up escaping to the kitchen.

It hadn't been until Robert left her that Jess had

realised she'd lost her spontaneity. Since arriving at Roseport she'd been busy trying to find it again. Sometimes on the way home at night she would just turn for the beach and she and Woody would picnic on fish and chips. She'd gone back to singing in the shower, and she and Woody loved to dance around the lounge room until they fell over with exhaustion.

Today's tennis had been exciting and exhilarating. She and Alex had faltered in the final round, but it didn't matter. Just watching him move fluidly around the court with the precision of a true sportsman had been prize enough.

'Hey, Jess.' Mick's partner Jenny grinned at her. 'There's a few blokes going to be disappointed tonight.'

Jess unplugged the hairdryer. 'Oh, well. Only one team can win.'

'Not the tennis, you dill.' Jenny laughed. 'I'm talking about the new doctor. The way he was looking at you all afternoon, I doubt anyone else will get to dance with you.'

Heat flooded her face. 'Don't be silly, Jenny. We work together, and he's only here for three months—well, less than that now.'

'Even so.' Jenny pulled open the door to leave. 'I know that look.' She walked away, chuckling.

Jess shook her head and smiled. She really was back at school camp, with women talking about who liked who. Leaning over the bathroom basin towards the mirror, she stroked on mascara and tried to dismiss Jenny's comments as silly gossip.

But the wondrous feeling of being in Alex's arms after they'd defeated Jenny and Mick kept snaking through her, going deeper and deeper, until she quivered with longing.

She shouldn't be feeling like this. She was a mother, a responsible citizen, a nurse and a pillar of the community. Yet all she could think about was being in his arms, tasting his hot and hungry kisses, and tumbling off the precipice she knew she teetered on.

Lust. That was all it was. Pure and simple. Well, she needed to get over it. She gripped the basin and blew out a long, slow breath.

She'd go to the cocktail party. Surrounded by a room full of people, she knew that nothing could happen between her and Alex. She would be safe from making a fool of herself. Then she'd go home and have a cold shower. If it worked for men, surely it worked for women too.

She spritzed on some perfume, dabbed lipgloss over her lipstick, and stepped out into the clubroom. The Ladies' Auxiliary had done a marvellous job decorating, and green and blue helium balloons tied with silver ribbon floated around the room. A live band played music and waiters carrying drinks mingled, looking smart in their black and white gear.

She saw Alex walking towards her, holding two flutes of champagne. His hair, still slightly damp from the shower, clung to the collar of his open-neck shirt. He grinned as he got close, white teeth against a tanned face. Her heart started hammering.

'Cheers.' He handed her a glass. 'Thanks for a great afternoon of tennis.'

'We didn't disgrace ourselves, did we?' She sipped the champagne, savouring the sensation of the bubbles fizzing in her mouth.

'Not at all. In fact, I'm glad I had you on my side. Facing you across the net would have been a bit scary.'

She laughed. 'Perhaps I need to bring my racquet to work, so I can scare you into completing the S2 forms properly.'

'Excuse me, Dr Fitzwilliam.' Myra Anderson from the Ladies' Auxiliary put her arm on his sleeve. 'Sorry to interrupt, but we thought if you presented the prizes now, we could then draw the raffle and everyone can just get on with having a good time.'

Alex raised his brows at Jess, as if saying, *Sorry, duty calls*, and let himself be led away by Myra.

Jess swallowed and squashed her disappointment. After all, she didn't have exclusive dibs on the man. He was here to encourage lots of donations towards the work of Medflight.

She moved back into the corner of the room to observe the awards. Alex made a witty speech, and then proceeded to congratulate the winners of each section. He shook all the winners' hands, but one of them, Alison Heppner, leaned in for a kiss.

Jess felt her smile tighten.

The crowd laughed and cheered, and Alex gave a wry grin. His job done, he stepped down and walked back to Jess.

Warmth filled her that he'd sought her out in such a large crowd.

Then Myra took to the podium. 'We are very fortunate here in Roseport to have the services of Medflight. It's one of those services we take for granted until we need it. But helicopters need a lot of money to operate, so we're thrilled to announce we have raised over five thousand dollars towards keeping Medflight in the air.'

Thunderous applause broke out and Myra eventually raised her hand for silence. 'Now, did you all pack an overnight bag and are you ready to leave? Because I am about to draw the winner of the *Tonight's the Night* raffle. 'The winner and a friend…' she gave a cheeky grin to the hoots from the crowd. '…will be leaving immediately in a chauffeur-driven limousine to be taken to The Seaspray at Ryeton, where they will enjoy an evening of Victorian splendour, with a sumptuous supper, a luxurious room, and a full buffet breakfast in the morning.'

Jess looked around with interest at the crowd. People leant forward in anticipation; couples gripped each other's hands, ever hopeful that their names would be pulled out of the hat for a night of romance. She suppressed a sigh. Sometimes the world seemed full of couples.

She hadn't bought a ticket—no point, really. She'd spent far too much money on another raffle—the one to win a selection of picture books which had been finalists in the Children's Book Council awards.

'And the winner is…'

Jess decided Myra loved the microphone—she was impersonating the MC's from movie award nights.

'Alex Fitzwilliam!'

The crowd started to clap. A stunned look streaked across Alex's face. Jess had a silent chuckle at his discomfiture.

Myra made her way over to him with the prize envelope, smiling widely. 'So, who are you taking with you, Doctor?'

Jess saw the sly look on Myra's face as her glance swept over her. Panic set in. Dread clawed at her. Surely he wouldn't ask her? Of *course* he wouldn't ask her. Did she *want* him to ask her?

Yes!

No!

She had her game plan for the evening, and it involved going home to her house for a date with a cold shower.

Alex tried to hand the envelope back. 'Thanks, Myra, but I think perhaps you should redraw the prize. Consider my tickets as a donation—or, better yet, auction them to raise more money.'

Jess relaxed. Thank goodness he was being sensible.

'Nonsense, Doctor. You won it fair and square.' The diminutive woman spoke briskly, wielding grey power. 'At least take Jess to supper.'

The crowd started to cheer and do a slow hand-clap.

Heat flooded Jess's face and she wanted to sink into the floor. The eyes of everyone she knew in town were zeroed in and watching her. Watching Alex.

Suddenly his arm curved around her waist, gripping her firmly. Spinning her around, he shepherded her to the door, out into the cool night air and into the waiting limousine.

CHAPTER SEVEN

Jess sank into the cool leather seats. Dread and panic slowly receded, and the irony of the situation took their place. The only non-couple of the night had won a romantic get-away. Laughter bubbled up and out. She couldn't stop it.

Alex sat down next to her, and a tingling sensation started in her toes and rapidly swept through her.

He waved out of the window as if he was a celebrity. 'If that's a friendly mob, I'd hate to be on the other side of them. I figured it best just to leave and give them what they wanted.'

With her ribs aching, Jess nodded, still unable to speak as waves of laughter kept rolling.

He dropped his arm and turned towards her, grinning. His dimples dug deeply into his cheeks, making him look younger than he was. Almost carefree. 'You know, this is the only raffle I've ever won. Usually it's a case of "What is it that I'm *not* going to win?"'

He laughed. 'I didn't even read what the prize was. Someone stuck a raffle book in my hand and I handed over the money. Besides, is there anyone who actually gets away with saying no to Myra?'

Jess pulled her laughter down to giggles. 'You poor thing. Harangued by the good women of Roseport.' She relaxed, enjoying the gentle teasing.

'Damn straight.' He put on a haughty voice. 'I've behaved above and beyond the call of duty.'

'I'll be sure to tell David so you get extra brownie points.'

Alex's emerald gaze swept lazily across her. 'So, you're up for supper?'

His voice, deeper than usual, encircled her, rolled across her, sparking a wave of shimmering heat that wove through her.

She swallowed. He'd been forced into this situation and he deserved an out. 'You really don't have to take me to supper. You could drop me off home and no one would be any wiser.'

'Don't you believe it. Myra will have spies.' He grinned again. 'I have to live in this town for a little while longer, you know.' He picked up her hand. 'Come to supper. It'll be fun.'

The heat of his hand travelled up her arm, setting off mini-explosions along the way until her breasts tingled. She should say no. But she'd enjoyed the day and she didn't want it to end just yet. Woody was safe at Anna's for the night, so she had no reason to dash home early.

And this surely counted as spontaneity? 'All right, you're on. But I'm paying.'

His laughter, warm like a cosy fire, enveloped her and

she leaned back, enjoying the unaccustomed luxury of the stretch vehicle.

Alex opened the champagne that had been provided, managing to pour two glasses without spilling a drop. 'It's an art.'

'And good suspension on the limo.'

'Hey, I worked as a barman while I was at med school.' The sparkle in his eyes tempered his feigned indignation.

Jess picked up a remote control. 'I wonder what this does?' She pressed a button and music surrounded them. She pressed the next one and a small television turned on.

Giggling like excited children, they pressed every button. Windows went up and down, lights came on and off, and climate control blasted out hot then cold air. The thirty-minute trip to Ryeton passed quickly.

The vehicle slowed and came to a stop. The chauffeur opened the door and they stepped out.

The Seaspray rose above them, a *grande dame* of Victorian style, restored to her former glory. Intricate iron lace verandas and arches bedecked her front, and a spectacular turret looked out to sea.

With his hand gently resting on her back, he guided her up the stairs into the foyer. The tessellated tiles beneath her feet told her she stood on a firm floor, yet it seemed to be shifting underneath her as she was pounded by an overload of sensations.

The heady perfume of stargazer lilies, the rainbow colours of the stained glass, the flickering lights of the chandeliers and the constant pressure of his hand on her back made the swirling and wondrous feelings in her veins more intense than ever before.

The highly polished mahogany reception desk gleamed, and Jess could see her reflection staring back at her, eyes large and cheeks flushed rose-red.

'Ah, Dr Fitzwilliam—welcome to The Seaspray.' The concierge tried to hand Alex a key. 'Douglas will take you to your room.'

Alex, his hand still gently resting on the curve of her waist, hesitated. 'Actually, we thought we'd start off with supper.'

'I see.' The man pursed his lips. 'I'm afraid supper in the Grand Dining Room isn't served until ten p.m., sir, which is another hour and a half away. Perhaps you would like to use the facilities in your room until then?'

The key hung between them in mid-air.

Alex glanced down at her, his eyes questioning. Was this what she wanted?

The concierge looked straight at her.

Oh, God, how had she got herself into this situation? People came to hotels to stay in rooms, not to linger in the foyer for ninety minutes.

She tried to think through the champagne-induced fuzz that had used to be her brain. Alone in a hotel room with Alex. Reality mimicking fantasy.

Well, they could take the key, get the concierge off their backs, have a brief peek at the room and then head down to the bar. That would be the most sensible way to manage the current embarrassing situation.

She gave a brief nod, and Alex took the proffered key.

Two minutes later Alex pushed open a heavy oak door and she stepped through onto carpet so plush it absorbed all sound.

Cream walls were hung with prints of seascapes by Australian artists, famous for painting Ryeton in the days of beach boxes and long piers. Two comfortable chairs sat separated by a mahogany table holding a cheese and fruit platter.

French doors opened out onto a veranda with a view of the ocean. The late-summer setting sun threw an orange glow onto the large king-size bed which dominated the room.

Alex walked up behind her, his breath caressing her ear. 'It's some room.'

She turned to face him. The tension, so much a part of him when he'd arrived in Roseport, had faded. Relaxation lines had replaced the stress ones, highlighting his high cheekbones. The ache to touch him intensified.

His eyes sparkled with amusement. 'We had to take the key or we'd have ruined the poor guy's day.'

She couldn't resist his boyish look. 'I guess most couples who stay here want to come upstairs first, their mind being on things other than food.'

Alex closed the small gap between them, his radiant heat washing over her, increasing her own temperature to almost boiling point. 'And what about us, Jess? What are our minds on?' His husky words fell into the void.

Her breath stalled. He knew. He knew exactly how she felt; she didn't need to tell him.

His finger gently traced a line from her eyebrow down her cheek and along her jaw.

White lights exploded in her head and she swayed towards him. Her hand cupped his face, her fingers exploring the rough and smooth of his cheek. She breathed in his scent of chamomile and sharp citrus.

'Jess, you're gorgeous; you drive me so crazy that I can't think straight. This current between us isn't lessening; it's building.'

She nodded. 'I know, I feel it too. But it's crazy.' The words tumbled out. 'You're only here for a short time, and I've got Woody to think about and—'

He put his fingers to her lips. 'Shh. I know that, Jess, but why does this need to be complicated? We're both adults. Do you think we can enjoy this now, knowing it can only last a few weeks?'

Her stomach turned over in shocked surprise. But slowly an idea started to form in her mind. 'So we could just have a fling based on lust?'

'Sure—if that's what you want to call it.' His mouth creased into a wicked smile. 'I think we could have fun together.'

An image of his lips on hers thundered through her. *Fun*. Wasn't being spontaneous and having some fun her new mantra? She'd always planned things. Planned to be a nurse, planned to marry Robert. All her planning had frayed in her hands, disappearing into nothingness.

Could she take what he offered, knowing there was an end in sight?

Woody.

She dropped her hand from his cheek.

He captured it inside his own, caressing her palm with his thumb. She struggled to think clearly as sweet pleasure invaded every corner of her body.

She might be about to go against everything she'd

ever believed in, but Woody needed absolute security. That was non-negotiable. 'Woody can't be hurt.'

His protective wall, absent for the last week, shot back into place. 'He won't be hurt. This would just be between me and you. Woody never has to get involved.'

A stab of pain shot through her at his bald words. The words stated what she already knew. But hearing them made them more real.

Loneliness clawed at her. She realised she'd been lonely for a long time—longer than the months since Robert had left her. She could walk away now or take what Alex offered—even though it was short-term.

Woody would be safe.

Nervously her tongue moistened her lips. 'I've never done anything like this before. I'm not even sure I know where to start.'

His eyes blurred with desire, darkening to the rich colour of green moss. 'We'll learn together.' His hand curved around the back of her neck. 'Are you absolutely sure about this?'

'Yes.' The word came out in whisper. She didn't want any more questions, any more opportunities to change her mind; she only wanted to be in his arms.

He laid her on the bed and gazed down at her.

She pulled him against her, his length moulding to her own, and he opened his mouth to hers.

She drank him in like a desert plant absorbing water. Reality exceeded her fantasies in every way. She savoured his taste—champagne mixed in with a heady fire of need.

A need she recognised. A need fuelled by failure. A need fuelled by loneliness.

Restraint was set loose, all hesitancy gone. They were two adults knowing what they wanted and taking it.

Her hands whipped under his shirt, exploring his back, absorbing the feel of his skin, feeling the way his muscles and bone connected. Committing it to memory.

He eased down the zipper on her dress and the underwired bodice fell away, exposing her breasts. The air felt cool against their aching heat.

She heard his sharp intake of breath as he kneeled, facing her.

'You're beautiful, Jess.' Alex whispered, pulling the dress over her head. It dropped to the floor with a swish of silk. Then, leaning forward, his hands cupped the soft creamy skin.

Her breasts tingled, their fullness resting in his hands. He started making long, lazy concentric circles until he reached her nipples, their height rising up to meet his thumbs.

Waves of wonder rose inside her. Heat built on heat. All thought slid away.

He lowered his mouth, enclosing one throbbing nipple, his tongue thrusting and teasing with deadly accuracy.

Pleasure sharp and pure shot through her, blasting all the way down to her toes. She wanted more of this. And she wanted him.

Her hands flew all over him, kneading his back, abrading his nipples with her thumbs, tugging at his belt, her fingers clumsy with need.

He moaned, a sound of overwhelming need. Rolling away from her, he finished what her hands couldn't do. 'These have to go.'

She hungrily watched him shuck his pants, seeing all of him for the first time, awesome in his beauty.

She opened her arms wide and he lay next to her, his breath hot on her face, his hands searing her skin, his fingers easing between her thighs.

Their gazes fused.

She heard the moan leave her lips as she moved against him, the spiral of pleasure threatening to explode. 'I need you now.'

He kissed her, his lips caressing her own. Then he moved over her, gently entering, letting her absorb him.

She arched up to take him, pushing forward, amazed at how right it felt, how well he fitted, as if he belonged.

They found their rhythm, driving each other higher and higher, until suddenly everything peaked and cascaded on top of them, spinning them out to the edge of reality before bringing them back together again.

'Thank you.' Alex's husky voice curled around her as he gathered her into his arms, his front cradling her back.

Cherished. The word popped into her head. She felt cherished, special. *Don't get used to it; you've only got a few short weeks.* The unwanted rational voice was back.

Ignoring it, she turned in his arms and faced him. 'So, about that supper you promised me?'

He glanced at his watch, then grinned at her, pure devilment lining his face. 'I'm afraid we've got another forty-five minutes to kill.' And he kissed her.

Squeals of happy children splashing in the waves filled the hot, humid air. Glad of his broad-brimmed hat and sunglasses, Alex glanced over at Jess as she patiently painted the noses of children with fluorescent zinc.

They'd been at the beach since ten this morning doing a Sunsmart health promotion—skin cancer awareness and a spot-check clinic. Jess still looked fresh, in a kaleidoscopic cotton dress which hung loosely over her, hiding every delectable curve of her body. Curves he'd explored and tasted over the last month. Curves he itched to touch.

And tonight he would take great pleasure in stripping off that dress and exploring her all over again. Tonight Jess was his. He didn't have to share her with anyone.

Finding time to be with her was harder than he'd thought. He had the time; she didn't. The reality was he was sharing Jess. Sharing her with her job, Roseport and Woody.

Ironically, all the things that drew him to her—her enthusiasm, her selflessness and her caring nature— were the things that kept her from him. She gave a lot of herself to people. He just wanted more for himself.

Damn, when had he become so selfish? *When Nick died.* The hollow voice inside his head which had gone quiet recently returned. *And you're taking more than you're giving.*

He breathed deeply. Jess was a grown woman. She'd agreed to the suggestion of a fling and she'd embraced their lovemaking. Hell, she'd even set the ground rules—so why did he feel like a heel?

Jess looked up from her sunscreen application and smiled at him. A smile blending passion with an air of concern.

There it was again. He knew she was worried at how he was coping surrounded by happy families on holiday. He waved back and gave her the thumbs-up. His chest hadn't tightened once. In fact, it hadn't since he'd told her about Nick.

He scanned the beach. The teenagers weren't heeding their message. The young kids wore tops and Lycra swimwear. But teenage girls baked themselves in skimpy bikinis, and shirtless boys with board shorts slung low on their hips paraded in the full sun. He noticed two girls further down the beach, trying to lift someone up.

Jess walked over, stepping under the shade of the awning. 'Phew, I'm hot.' Pulling a cold drink out of the fridge box, she tilted her head back and rolled the can up and down her neck.

Memories of trailing kisses along that delectable neck slammed into him. Tonight he would revisit her slender neck, explore her pulse-points, and kiss every square inch of creamy skin.

'So, how's the spot-check clinic going?' She tugged the ring pull on the can and took a long drink.

'I've diagnosed a few solar keratoses and arranged to see them tomorrow at the clinic. I'll treat them with cryotherapy. The clinic's got a handheld liquid nitrogen unit, hasn't it?'

'Yes, we've got one. I'll make sure it's ready to go for you tomorrow.'

'Thanks.' He glanced at his watch. Three hours until his working day was over and his time with Jess could begin. 'All set for tonight?' Had he really said that? He sounded like an excited kid, asking if someone was still coming over to play.

'Did we have plans?' Her feigned look of innocence disintegrated into laughter as she scooped up some ice and moved to stuff it down his shirt. 'Just cooling you off, Doctor.'

He caught her hands too late and the ice hit his hot skin. He pulled her in close, loving the feel of her in his arms, the undefinable feeling he always got when she was beside him.

Her look steadied him and he dropped her hands. 'Enough frivolity, Nurse Henderson. Back to work.'

A yell on the beach made them both turn. The two girls he'd seen earlier were trying to walk a young man over to them. Slung between them, he was barely walking.

Alex jogged over. 'What's up, girls?'

'He's gone all weird, and he says he feels awful.' Panting, the taller girl continued, 'He keeps kinda zoning out.'

Alex put his arm under the young man's shoulder to support him. 'What's your name, mate?'

The youth tilted his head sideways, as if he was having trouble focussing. 'Tim.'

Jess appeared beside him. 'Heatstroke?'

'Could be. Help me get him over to the shade.'

Together they managed to walk Tim over to the tent and lie him down on the massage table they used as a portable examination table. He immediately rolled on his side into the foetal position, pulling his knees up toward his chin. He started dry-retching.

The girls squealed.

Jess grabbed a bucket and supported Tim.

Alex groaned internally. 'Thanks for bringing him over, girls. Can you just wait under the trees for a bit while we get Tim sorted?'

'Sure—will he be all right?' Anxiety lined their faces.

'We'll work out what's wrong with him and keep you posted.' He turned back to see Jess wiping Tim's face with a towel moistened with the cold water from the melted ice.

'His temp's forty. He needs to go over to the clinic so we can cool him down.'

Tim let out a long, low moan.

'Tim, does it hurt anywhere?' Alex voiced the question.

'Me gut.' He gripped his stomach.

He checked Tim's pupils, which were dilated and sluggish. He examined his skin. There was no sign of sunburn. Still, you could get heatstroke without being sunburnt. A nagging unease dragged at him.

He took Tim's pulse, then checked his air entry with a stethoscope. 'He's extremely tachypnoeic and sweaty.'

'Both signs of heatstroke.' Jess reached for the emergency bag. 'Do you want an IV to counter the dehydration?'

He keeps kinda zoning out. The words of one of the girls hammered in his head.

'Alex? The IV?' Jess raised her brows, requesting confirmation.

'Yes—thanks. You insert it, and then cover him with as many damp towels as you can. I'm just going to have a quick chat with the girls who brought Tim in. Back in a minute.'

Ignoring Jess's surprised look, he walked over to the girls. 'How long has Tim been at the beach?'

The taller girl replied. 'Not that long. Twenty minutes, maybe. Why?'

'Just wondering if he'd been lying in the sun for a long time.' Alex formed his next question carefully. 'There's a big group of you here today—a pre-uni party?'

'Sort of. More like post-schoolies. We've come for the music festival.' Both girls giggled. 'We're just taking a break at the beach before heading back for the night set.'

'Sounds like fun.' He kept his voice casual. 'Do you think Tim might have taken something to add to the fun before coming down here?' He scanned their faces for any reaction to his question.

Their gazes slid away from his face, their demeanour changing rapidly. One of them dragged her toe through the sand before looking up again.

Alex spoke quietly, gently. 'It's important I know so I can treat him properly.'

The taller girl dragged in a breath and looked at her friend. 'He might have popped an E.'

MethyleneDioxyMethAmphetamine. Ecstasy. He swallowed the expletive that rose to his lips.

'Alex—come quickly.' Jess's frantic voice shot through him.

He ran back, his long legs covering the short distance in a moment. 'What's up?'

'He's fitting.' Jess was tilting Tim's chin, trying gently to insert a Guedel airway into his mouth, as well as acting as a shield to keep him from falling off the massage table. His shuddering body twitched hard against her.

'He needs Diazepam.' Alex put his hands on the youth's twitching legs.

'I've got some in my kit. You hold Tim, he's too heavy for me, and I'll draw up the Diazepam.'

They swapped positions. 'He's taken Ecstasy. Thank goodness you got that IV in.'

'Oh, jeez.' Jess snapped the top off the familiar brown ampoule. 'You suspected something, didn't you? I thought it was just heatstroke.'

He nodded, still concentrating on restraining Tim from injury. 'Give the ten milligrams over two minutes.'

Jess plunged the needle into the rubber bung and slowly administered the drug.

His fitting eased and finally Tim lay still and unconscious, but breathing.

Alex grabbed his phone and dialled 000. He ordered an ambulance and then, ringing off, he turned to Jess. 'This is becoming a habit. I'm going to string David up when he gets back. This practice is a litany of emergencies.'

'I think it's been an unusually dramatic summer.' She gave a wry smile. 'But you have to admit it floats your boat more than insurance medicine.'

A tremor of surprise rocked through him. The thought of returning to that mind-numbing work made his mouth go dry. How had she worked that out before he had?

'What can we do while we wait for the ambulance?' Her brown eyes, wide with worry, gave her a vulnerable look.

'Nowhere near enough. He's at risk of kidney failure and disseminated intravascular coagulation. Not to mention brain haemorrhage and liver damage. He needs to be in Intensive Care an hour ago.'

He sighed. 'So we keep his airway open, cool him down as much as we can, monitor his breathing and put two litres of IV saline into him, *stat*. And pray.'

'Will he be OK?' A timid voice sounded behind him.

He turned to see the girls anxiously waiting. 'I don't know.' He ran his hand through his hair. 'This is what taking drugs can do. It can kill you. No high is worth the risk.'

Jess put her hand briefly on his arm, giving it a supportive squeeze, and then brushed past him. 'Girls, we need to contact Tim's next of kin. Who do we call? His parents? Do you have their number?'

'We really don't know him that well, but he's got a mobile—we left it on his towel. He'll have numbers in that.'

Jess turned back. 'Are you all right for now? I'll go and sort out contacting his next of kin.'

She stood in front of him, calm, in control, gorgeous and desirable. He looked at the time. Four o'clock. He did a quick calculation of the distance to Ryeton, time for a handover and time for catching a ride back to Roseport.

Tonight could still work. He'd *make* it work. 'I'll have to go on the ambulance with him so, I'll meet you back here?'

'OK. I'll probably still be packing up by the time you get back.'

The thought of his evening with Jess kept Alex going right through Tim's touch-and-go ambulance ride and admission to Intensive Care.

He left Tim fully ventilated and sedated, being vigorously cooled by chilled IV infusions and cold packs, and with his urine output being measured hourly and monitored for blood.

The only bright spot of the entire experience was the buzz he'd got from being back in an Intensive Care Unit as part of a medical team.

Hot and tired, he made it back to the beach around six. Most of the families had headed home for tea. In the distance he saw the Community Health expo gear had been packed up, the display boards resting in a pile under the Norfolk pines.

Jess would be waiting. For him. Just for him. His blood heated at the thought.

He'd take her straight back to the house. He had a selection of fresh seafood in the fridge—crayfish, oysters, and Moreton Bay bugs. They'd eat on the deck overlooking Roseport Bay, sip champagne, and talk.

He loved talking to her. Penny had never really been interested in his work and had certainly never read any journal articles. But it was more than work; Jess had an interest in so many different things.

And after talking there was the outdoor spa, and—

His thoughts came to an abrupt halt. Jess sat on the sand cuddling a redheaded child, her head bent close to his.

Woody.

CHAPTER EIGHT

A STRANGE sensation washed over Alex at the picture Jess and Woody made. Funny, he'd never really pictured Jess and her nephew together as a family. He tended to compartmentalise them in his mind, thinking of them as two single units.

This was only the second time he'd seen them together. And now Woody was on the beach in Jess's lap, looking for all the world as if he belonged there.

His heart contracted.

Jess glanced up as he approached and scrambled to her feet, frowning. Woody clung to her legs. 'Oh, I'm so glad you're back. I've been trying to ring you but the mobile network is clogged due to the music festival.'

She ran her hand through Woody's hair in a soothing manner. 'Things have gone a bit pear-shaped since you left. The music festival has its own medical support, but the nurse up there hasn't had a break all day because her relief didn't show up.

'She's at her wits' end, exhausted, and she's asked me if I can give her an hour so she can at least eat dinner.' She looked apologetic. 'I really couldn't say no. She's helped us out in the past, and in the country that's what you do.'

He sighed, disappointment sliding through him. 'Oh, well, not to worry. It's just another delay in a very long day. Go on, take Woody to the babysitter's and head up to the festival. I'll have dinner waiting for you at my place when you've finished.'

'It's not quite as simple as that, Alex.' Her words sent a ripple of concern through him.

Anxiety mingling with determination crossed her face. 'Anna's come down with a migraine, so she's at home lying in the dark, waiting for the painkillers to kick in.'

He spoke slowly, realisation dawning. 'And she was going to mind Woody?'

'Yes.'

The word hovered between them, loaded with meaning.

She wrung her hands and looked at him, her eyes large and imploring, her teeth gnawing her bottom lip. 'I don't want to ask you this, but I don't have a choice. Can you please mind Woody for an hour?'

A chill ran along his warm skin. He hadn't minded a child since Nick's death. He looked at her beautiful face, taut with unease and worry, and saw how much it had cost her to ask. She'd been adamant she wanted to keep Woody separate from their affair. She wouldn't have asked if she'd had an alternative.

He looked down at the little boy with colouring so similar to his own and yet so different from Nick. 'I suppose Woody and I will survive an hour.'

Relief filled her eyes. 'Thank you.' She bent down to Woody. 'Woody, this is Dr Alex. Do you remember?

He's going to play with you on the beach while I go to work. I promise I won't be very long, and we'll have an ice cream when we get back.'

The kid was going to get ice cream. He wondered what *he* would get.

Alex knelt down to Woody's level and a pair of sky-blue eyes appraised him sharply. 'Hello, Woody.'

The child clung to Jess's legs like a limpet suctioned to a rock. Immovable.

Great start! He wasn't thrilled to be minding Woody, and Woody wasn't thrilled at being minded. Hell, the kid had only even met him once, very briefly, so he didn't blame him.

Distraction had always worked well with Nick. He picked up a handful of sand, letting the grains trail through his fingers. 'Can you show me how you fill your bucket with sand?'

'Sandcastles.' Woody broke away from Jess and ran over to his bucket.

Jess's smile full of grateful thanks washed over him, warming him, making him feel slightly happier about the situation. 'He's had his dinner, so—'

Go, he mouthed at her. Better for her to leave while Woody was occupied. He'd deal with any fall-out. The beach offered a myriad of distractions.

Jess gave a wave and ran to her car.

Woody continued to dig furiously, with single-minded intent. Each scoop of sand was carefully moved across and then tipped into his large bucket.

Alex sprawled out on a beach towel, lying on his front with his head resting in his hands, keeping Woody firmly in his sights. At least the kid seemed to be keeping himself occupied. This could work out just fine. He'd sit and watch, and Woody would play.

'Scuffy.'

A plastic tugboat landed next to his head, spraying him with sand.

''Lex play Scuffy.' Woody plopped down beside him, his small hands pulling at his shirt.

He looked into a pair of vivid blue eyes filled with quiet determination. He recognised that look. The 'I-know-what-I-want-and-I'm-not-budging-until-I-get-it' look. It had been a favourite of Nick's.

Woody would pester him until he played, and withstanding his persistence would take more energy than just giving in to the inevitable. Resignation filled him and he stood up.

'OK, mate, let's play with Scuffy.' He kicked off his shoes. 'You pull him along in the water, and I'll load him up with periwinkles.' He followed Woody down to the shallows.

Late! The word pounded in Jess's head as she changed through the gears, negotiating the winding road back down to the coast from the festival. To appease the locals the festival was being held ten minutes out of town on a farm. Slowing to forty kilometres, she changed down into second and took a sharp curve.

How had Woody coped with yet another person minding him? Sometimes she hated needing to work, putting Woody into childcare, but they had to live.

How had Alex coped, looking after Woody?

His look—reluctance mixed with fear and overlaid with pain—when she'd asked him to mind Woody had played across her mind for the last seventy-five minutes. Woody was probably the first child he'd spent time with since Nick's death.

She'd hated putting both Alex and Woody in a difficult situation.

Five minutes later she pulled into the beach car park. A cool breeze had sprung up, and only a few hardy souls braved the conditions. She scanned the beach, looking for two redheads.

She squinted against the low sun and anxiety skated along her veins. Where were they? She looked in the opposite direction. Not there either.

A surge of panic flooded her. What if Alex hadn't coped? She should never have put him in that situation—never have asked him to mind Woody. She should have said no to the festival nurse, put Woody's needs first.

'Jess!'

She spun around at the sound of Woody's voice. He was running towards her across the grass. Alex followed a pace behind, holding three ice creams.

She scooped Woody up, hugging him tightly.

'Down.' Woody squirmed in her arms. 'Please.'

She set him down, trying to ignore the jab of disappointment that he hadn't wanted a cuddle.

Alex handed Woody his ice cream. 'There you go, mate.' He caught Jess's gaze, his eyes crinkling with laughter at her expression. 'A boy with an ice cream has no time for cuddles—didn't you know that?'

'I guess I'm still learning.' She ignored the swirl of longing his grin elicited.

'Here you go; ice cream is good for soothing a battered soul.' He handed her a waffle cone filled with boysenberry vanilla swirl, and sank down onto the grass.

'Thanks.' Jess licked the ice cream, savouring the flavour on her tongue. 'Sorry I'm late.' She sat down next to Woody, who was now happily eating in between her and Alex.

He shrugged. 'Fifteen minutes after the expected time is still on time in my book.'

'Ah, well, that would be the difference between doctors and nurses.' She grinned. 'Our clock ticks to a different beat.'

He raised his brows. 'Them's fighting words, Nurse Henderson. I'll remind you of that next time your Pap Test clinic runs late.'

Jess studied him while she ate her ice cream, hiding her gaze behind the enormous waffle cone. Fatigue lines were etched around his eyes, and his end-of-day stubble gave him a rakish look. But the furrowed brow lines and the tension that often clung to him were missing.

'Thanks, Alex. Thanks for minding Woody. I know it can't have been easy.'

He paused mid-bite of ice cream and hooked his gaze to hers. 'People help each other in the country, Jess. It's what you do.'

Disappointment rammed into her, confusing her. What had she wanted him to say? *Oh, that's fine, Jess. It's been fun. I'll mind Woody any time.*

Alex had done his duty. He'd helped her out—helped out a friend.

And, heavens, hadn't she been juggling things these last few weeks to keep the two men in her life totally separate? She'd been protecting both of them. Woody and Alex didn't belong together. She knew that. So why did she feel so cheated by Alex's reaction?

Alex broke the silence that hovered between them. 'I better call in and check if Anna needs anything for her migraine. I'll see you at work in the morning.' He stood up. 'Bye-bye, Woody.'

Woody's ice-cream-covered face looked up at Alex. 'Bye-bye.'

Jess watched him walk away, leaving her with an empty feeling that ached in a way she'd never known. She hauled Woody against her and hugged him tight.

The antiseptic hospital smell hit Jess's nostrils, bringing back a flood of memories. Funny how working in hospital seemed so long ago—and yet it had been only a few months.

She and Alex had driven over to Ryeton because three of their patients were being discharged. Good discharge planning meant a smooth transition for everyone—even if it ate up a chunk of time. Discharge meetings would absorb the morning.

Alex, like David, had Wednesday afternoons off, so she was looking forward to having the clinic to herself and catching up on a myriad of unfinished tasks.

Alex paused and let Jess walk through the ward doorway first. She loved the way his impeccable manners made her feel as if she was the only woman in the world—even though she knew he would have ushered any woman through the door first.

'Mrs Romanski.' Alex stepped up to the bed and picked up the elderly woman's hand. Bending close, he spoke loudly in her ear as she was quite deaf but refused to wear her hearing aid. 'How are you feeling today?'

'I am very good, Doctor, now you have come.' Her rheumy eyes sparkled and she seemed to sit up higher in the bed.

Jess bit her lip so she wouldn't smile. She imagined what a flirt Mrs Romanski would have been sixty years ago. She'd noticed how many of the elderly women batted their eyes at Alex. But it wasn't just flirting with a handsome man. He had a knack of making his patients feel special, as if he had all the time in the world for them.

'Mrs Romanski, I want you to meet Jess Henderson. She's our nurse and will visit you at home—check your dressing and teach you how to do your blood sugar tests.'

Jess stepped forward to say hello, but Mrs Romanski didn't look at her.

'Are you not going to visit me too, Doctor?' Her Hungarian accent was still evident, even after years in Australia.

Jess decided the woman had a degree in flirting.

Alex kept his face straight. 'I'll be visiting once a week, and Jess will be coming once a day.' He drew the sheet up over the bed cradle. 'Now, let's have a look at this wound.'

Jess moved in to observe the wound, standing close to Alex, her sleeve brushing his. *How close do you actually have to stand to him? She's eighty-two. Get a grip—you don't have to mark your territory. Remember, he's only yours for a short time.*

The voice hammered in Jess's head. Just lately the voice had become far too persistent. She didn't want to think about the time after Alex had left Roseport. She only wanted to think about now, and enjoying the time they had left.

Jess peered at the ulcer. The edges were clean after being debrided, and it was slowly granulating. Keeping a close eye on Mrs Romanski's diabetes could only help it continue to improve.

'Has the physio been in to see you?' Jess smiled at her patient.

'Yes, I have my new walking frame. Very nice, with a blue seat.' She turned to Alex. 'It matches my eyes.'

Jess ploughed on. 'That's great. Walking is going to help your ulcer heal. I'll visit you at your home tomorrow, around noon.'

The older lady gave her a curt nod, her only recognition of having heard the last remark.

'Right, Mrs Romanski, I'll see you next week—unless Jess feels you need to see me sooner. I'll ask the ward nurse to come in and dress the ulcer.' Alex put the cover back over the cradle. 'You have a good trip home.' Alex stepped back from the bed.

'Thank you, Doctor. I look forward to your visit.'

She waved as Jess and Alex walked out of the door.

Two more discharge visits, more flirting than a group of teenage girls at a dance, and their morning was finished. Alex opened the car door for Jess.

'I had no idea you were such a pin-up boy amongst the grey-power set.' Jess sat down in the car and fastened her seat belt.

He grinned as he hopped in next to her. 'That's me. Chick magnet for the over seventies.' He turned the key in the ignition. Throwing his arm casually behind her seat's headrest, he reversed out of the parking space and headed the car towards Roseport. He flicked on the CD player and jazz filled the car.

She breathed in deeply and relaxed, enjoying the music, enjoying being so close to him in a confined space, and savouring his scent of citrus mixed with sunshine. She loved to watch him: how the tendons of his hands moved as he gripped the wheel, the way a fine line of blond stubble roughened his jaw, and his unconscious action of adjusting his sunglasses by pushing them up to the bridge of his nose. She drank it all in, ignoring the ticking clock in her head.

'You've been quiet.' Alex smiled. 'Stop thinking about work; it's lunchtime.'

His words roused her. 'Ha! It's all right for some; you've got the afternoon off. The rest of us have to work.'

'Paperwork—which can always wait.' He dropped his hand onto her thigh. 'What if I give you the afternoon off?'

Trying to ignore the flickers of longing that ran straight up her leg, she lifted his hand and put it back on the steering wheel. She was determined to keep work separate from their affair. 'Technically, you can't actually do that. David is my boss.'

'Hmm, that's tricky—because I gave Anna the afternoon off, and she didn't mention the lack of protocol. She's taking calls on her mobile and paging me if I'm required.' He pulled the car off the main road and headed down towards the breakwater. 'I think it's time you played Wednesday afternoon hooky with me.'

A tremor of excitement ran through her. She raised her brows at him. 'Golf's not my game.'

'Cheeky.' His mouth curved upwards in a wicked smile, promising sultry kisses and long, languid touching. 'I have no intention of playing golf.'

The ever-present banked heat deep inside her roared into life. She felt daring and carefree.

He pulled the car into the Parkinsons' driveway. Hopping out quickly, he strode around the car and opened her door. Taking her hand, he helped her out of the car and into his arms.

'Do you think you can push through your work ethic and take the afternoon off?' His eyes, hungry with desire, scanned her face. 'I promise I'll make it worth your while.' His deep voice caressed her.

Her blood swirled in eddies of longing. 'I'm sure you'll try your best.' She pulled away from him, laughing, and ran around to the back of the house, knowing he would chase her. Knowing that to be out of sight of the neighbours was the best place to be. She didn't need all of Roseport talking. Or the Parkinsons being told.

He caught up with her on the back deck. 'Playing chasey, are we?' He caught her around the waist and gently pulled her through the back door and into his arms

She giggled at the joy of being caught. 'Leaving the

back door open? You really have got into the spirit of country living.'

'Hmm.' Alex trailed kisses along the hollow of her neck.

Rockets of tingling, shuddering pleasure washed through her and her nipples hardened against the lace of her bra. She ran her fingers through his hair, feeling the curls tangle around her fingers.

She gave up on repartee and gave in totally to his kisses, drowning in the delicious sensations he elicited.

He remembered everything she enjoyed: butterfly kisses across her eyelids, sweet kisses along her cheeks, and deep, fire-hot kisses on her mouth.

She gave up on restraint. She wanted him, no matter the time of day, no matter that she should be at work. He'd be leaving soon enough. Didn't she deserve this now?

Too many days had passed since her fingers had skimmed across his skin, since her lips had explored his body, since he'd made her almost weep with the wonder of his touch.

She unbuttoned his shirt, one button at a time, trailing kisses along his chest, each one lower than the last. She savoured the salty taste of his skin. Each kiss driving away the ticking clock in her head.

His hands tightened on her scalp at her touch. He loosened the band around her hair, releasing the long strands so they cascaded down her back. 'I love your hair.'

He pulled her close, his body pressing against her, his arousal hard against her thigh. She gloried in the knowledge that she did this to him, that his need for her was as strong as her own.

'I want you in my bed, where I can see all of you, feel all of you.' Holding her hand, he walked her into the bedroom.

Slowly, they undressed each other. As each item of clothing was discarded the newly exposed skin was kissed, tasted and explored, until neither of them could take another moment of torturous restraint.

Pushing at his shoulders, she rolled him onto his back and lowered herself down onto him, desperate to have him enter her and make her whole.

He filled her, his power vibrating against her, driving her need, sending it spiralling up until it cascaded over them both.

She gripped him to her, wanting to melt into him, to be a part of him, never separate again.

He completed her. She needed him as she needed air. He infused her with joy and a love of life. Without him everything was grey and listless.

Snuggling in against him, she let his shelter and protection encase her in delicious warmth.

A perfect moment. She loved him.

A chill shuddered through her. Her stomach lurched. Oh, God, she loved him.

How had she let this happen? They'd agreed to a fling. An affair with a time limit. Love and commitment were not part of the package.

She'd told herself she *couldn't* love him, because he was only in Roseport for a short time, because he didn't want another serious relationship and because she was never falling for the wrong man again.

Never falling for a man who couldn't love Woody.

But they had all been false defences. She loved him. All of him. The caring doctor, the wondrous lover, the lost and grieving father, even the wounded man who shied away from commitment and children.

He'd invaded her heart and her life. He'd made himself part of her.

And he was leaving in three weeks.

Flashes of her life in Roseport before Alex had arrived whipped through her mind, reminding her of her loneliness. Memories of the long nights she had lain awake, feeling so very alone, knowing she would be raising Woody on her own.

Now she knew that it had been a life of existing. And there was so much more to life than that.

Her heart contracted and she fought back the well of tears that filled her eyes.

Alex's arms tightened around her. She never wanted to leave the security of those arms. And she didn't have to. Not yet.

She had three weeks—twenty-one days, five hundred and four hours—left to spend with him. And she would live every second, immerse herself in him and create memories to last a lifetime.

CHAPTER NINE

ALEX sipped his latte as he walked along the main street. Jess was right; The Provedore did have the best coffee in town.

He dodged a few kids racing along the footpath ahead of their parents, who strolled casually behind them, enjoying the slower pace of their weekend away.

Alex smiled at their pleasure. Surprise trickled through him. A few weeks ago a family's pleasure would have caused him pain. But not today. Today the sun was out and he was making the most of what was left of his day.

The Saturday clinic, technically a morning clinic, had been a litany of excited kids gone wrong. He'd plastered a broken arm after a ten-year-old boy had come off second best with a kite in a tree, removed a sultana that had been shoved a very long way up a nostril, and he'd stitched a cut hand, injured when a fish-filleting knife slipped.

By the time he'd finished up it had been late afternoon. Now he was out enjoying a leisurely stroll while he could. He never knew when he would be called for an emergency.

He glanced in shop windows, checked out house prices in the real estate agents' windows, and found himself outside the toy shop, staring at a display of beach toys.

There was a little red boat with two sailors, very similar to Woody's boat. The boat he'd insisted Alex play with. The memory of the hour or so he'd spent with Woody had been popping up in his mind with increasing frequency.

He smiled at the memory. Woody had organised him to build a sand fort with a moat so he could sail Scuffy. And they'd collected the most enormous collection of periwinkles, which had almost sunk the small plastic boat.

When they'd walked over to the milk bar for ice cream, Woody had pointed out trees and birds and cars, keeping up a continuous monologue. Life through a child's eyes was refreshingly simple.

Woody's boat didn't have any sailors, and Alex was sure they'd add to Woody's games—especially as they had their own rescue rings. They could float safely if the periwinkles sank the boat. He wondered if they were sold separately. He moved to walk into the shop.

He stopped abruptly.

What the hell was he doing? He shook his head to clear it. Woody had nothing to do with him—so what the hell was he doing, thinking of buying him a gift?

Woody wasn't Nick.

And Jess would have a fit if he bought Woody something. Apart from that one evening on the beach she'd kept Woody separate. Which suited him. He didn't want a child in his life; he didn't want to become involved. He had exactly what he wanted, didn't he?

He shoved the empty feeling inside him even deeper.

He only had two short weeks before David returned. Two weeks left with Jess before he had to head back to Melbourne.

Melbourne.

Three hours' drive from Roseport.

The thought unsettled him. He shoved his hands in his pockets and started walking quickly. He didn't want to think about any of it. Not about Jess, not about Woody, or the boring job that waited for him. His safe job.

He needed to clear his head. A run along the beach would do the trick.

Ten minutes later he shoved his phone in the pocket of his running kit and jogged down the back garden and out onto the beach. The low tide exposed hard, wet sand, perfect for running. Salt stung his nostrils. His mind shifted into neutral as he absorbed the sights and sounds of the beach. Gulls squawked and circled, pelicans followed the fishing boats as they approached the pier, and children's shouts hung on the early evening air.

He gave himself up to the physical demands of the run, pushing his body to its limits. His chest burned, his leg muscles stung, and slowly a blessed numbness entered his body and mind, silencing his unsettling thoughts.

Nearing the pier, he had to slow to avoid the children playing in the shallows. He didn't want to slow down. He wanted to run hard, wanted to totally exhaust himself. Frustrated, he cut up the beach towards the Norfolk pines and a clear run home.

The enticing smell of freshly cooked fish and chips penetrated his nostrils. He swung around to locate the source.

Jess.

His already pounding heart kicked up a notch.

She sat on a picnic rug, looking as gorgeous as always, her sunglasses giving her an air of sophistication at odds with the down-to-earth woman he knew. She was opening a large white bundle of fish and chips.

Jess always spent Saturdays with Woody. The thought rocked through him, and he looked around for the little redheaded boy and his Scuffy.

Suddenly Woody jumped up from behind Jess, his face glowing with excitement at the prospect of fish and chips. Jess gave him a quick cuddle.

A cosy warmth glowed inside him at the picture they made. Mother and child together.

Woody looked up and saw him, a smile splitting his face. He started running, his chubby legs carrying him straight to Alex. ''Lex—chips!''

A flicker of delight spluttered inside him at Woody's enthusiasm at seeing him. 'Hey, matey. Chips, eh?' He tousled his hair.

Woody's hand grabbed his running shorts, tugging him towards the picnic rug and Jess. 'Come on.'

He couldn't see Jess's eyes behind her sunglasses. Did she want him here with Woody? Would her maternal instincts push him away? His gut churned. Did he want that?

'It seems you're being invited to join us.' She gave him a wry smile.

'It looks that way, doesn't it?' He shrugged his shoulders, not knowing what else to say, feeling as if he was imposing and yet wanting to be there, picnicking with them both.

'Chippies, Jess. Chippies.' Woody plonked down, beaming with anticipation.

Alex sat down to catch his breath.

'Hard run?' Jess smiled and passed him a water bottle. 'You look hot and thirsty.' Resting on her knees, she ripped off a section of the white paper and placed some chips and fish in front of Woody. Pulling open a travel-cup, she set it down next to them. 'Chips and a drink—eat up.'

Alex blinked. He'd heard Jess talk about Woody, experienced her protective side, seen her anxiety the night he'd minded Woody, but he'd never really seen her in full-on, organising, practical mothering mode. He thought of her in terms of the pleasure she gave to him, her beauty, her laugh, her passion for life. Something about her kneeling in front of Woody rocked him to his core.

His Madonna and her child. The thought stunned him.

She turned to him. 'Dig in, there's plenty. But make sure you leave a potato cake for me.'

Her words grounded him, bringing his attention back to the food. If he concentrated on the food he would be fine. He'd eat and leave. 'Potato cake fiend, are you?'

She licked her fingers and her eyes danced. 'It's my only vice.'

Heat shot to his groin. He wanted to haul her into his arms.

She grinned. 'There's local scallops and flake, so take your pick.' She tucked some stray hair behind her ear and bit into a scallop. Juice dribbled down her chin.

'Oh, I'm hopeless on picnics.' She tried to lick it up with her tongue, looking like a child.

The heat inside him burned. He grabbed a serviette and, moving closer, wiped her mouth. As he did, he bent his head lower to steal a kiss.

Suddenly Woody scrambled under his arm, knocking him backwards. 'My turn.' Woody grabbed the serviette from his hand and wiped Jess's mouth too. 'I helped.' He beamed at them both.

Alex tried to keep a straight face. 'You did. You were a big help. Thanks, mate.' Alex could feel Jess shaking with laughter next to him. 'Now you've finished helping, how about you sit down and finish eating your chips?'

Hell, where had that bit of parenting come from? Perhaps the skill never left—like riding a bike. But he didn't want to remember how to parent. Being Nick's dad had been his greatest achievement. And he'd lost that when he'd lost Nick.

'Play Scuffy?' A hopeful tone filled Woody's voice.

'After you've eaten your chips.' He suppressed a curse at the parenting words that fell so effortlessly from his lips.

'OK.' Woody happily tucked in.

After the last chip had disappeared, Jess leaned back and stretched, patting her tummy. 'There's something about eating fish and chips on the beach that makes them taste *so* much better.'

His eyes zeroed in on the expanse of exposed skin between her T-shirt and the waistband of her shorts.

A dog barked in the distance.

Woody jumped up and clambered across Alex's lap, trying to get to Jess. 'Where's dog?'

Alex instinctively brought his arms up around the scared child, hugging him to his chest, feeling the child's pounding heart against his own.

Round eyes filled with fear looked up at him, and fingers with the grip of superglue sank into his neck.

Jess reached out for Woody. 'It's OK, Woody. The dog isn't near you.'

Alex met her concerned gaze. He gently turned Woody around to face the other direction, still keeping him in his lap. 'Look over there, mate.' He pointed towards the dog. 'Can you see the dog on the lead? His owner is taking him for a walk.'

'Dog made a big noise.' Woody snuggled into him, as he peered at the dog in the distance.

The warmth of the little boy's body seeped into him, spreading out in an almost comforting heat. 'He did. He was doing dog talk. The dog won't hurt you.'

He suddenly found his arms had tightened around the child in a protective way. Unease wove through him and he dropped his arms.

Jess put her arms out towards Woody and he crawled into her lap.

Cool air rushed into the place where Woody's warm body had rested, bringing with it a sense of loss.

Jess hugged Woody and dropped a kiss on his head. 'Do you want to build a sandcastle?'

He shook his head. 'No. Want to play Scuffy with 'Lex.' All thoughts of the dog had disappeared.

'Right, then.' Alex stood up happy to be busy, happy not to think about how good it had felt to cuddle Woody. He pulled Jess up with him, enjoying the sensation of her fingers gripping his arm. 'If I have to play Scuffy, then so do you.'

'You're on.' She tossed her hair and grinned. 'But you boys will have to catch me first.' She turned on her heel and raced off down the beach, sand flying.

Woody chased Jess, his stout little legs churning through the sand, his arms pumping by his side.

Jess slowed and turned around to face them, jogging backwards, waving, teasing.

As Alex and Woody got closer she gave them a 'come-and-get-me' look, turned and ran again.

Her cheeky grin and flushed cheeks spurred Alex on. He swept Woody up onto his shoulders and chased after her.

Woody's delighted shrieks rent the air.

Holding Woody steady with one arm, Alex reached out and grabbed Jess's T-shirt. He pulled her back towards him and she stumbled, collapsing on the soft sand.

Dropping to his knees, Alex leaned over her and swung Woody off his shoulders onto the sand. As Woody's feet touched the ground, Alex over-balanced and sprawled on top of Jess, pinning her under him.

Woody scrambled onto his back.

Jess's laughter rippled around him.

'Gotcha.' He swept his lips gently across hers, savouring her special taste. Her energy rushed through him, vibrating with life, filling him with joy.

Arms encircled him. Long, shapely arms. Small, chubby arms. Both giving warmth and love. Peace flooded him, filling the dark crevices deep inside him with a healing balm.

Contentment soothed and lulled him. Nothing existed outside of those arms. He gave himself up to the experience, welcoming the love that surrounded him.

No!

Reality rushed back with the force of a king tide. The loving arms which had soothed suddenly choked. Gulping in air like a man suffocating, he rolled away.

He *couldn't* feel like this. He refused to accept these feelings. Refused to accept this love. He didn't belong here. He'd stuffed up his marriage and lost his son. He wasn't doing that again. He wasn't ever going to be a father again.

Jess's laughter faded. She sat up, her brow furrowed and her almond eyes filled with confusion.

And love.

Hell, how had this happened? This was supposed to have been a fling—fun and good times, with no ties.

'Are you OK?' Jess sounded worried.

His phone rang, the sound piercing the tension that surrounded them. He punched the green key, thankful for the diversion.

A minute later he rang off. 'Sorry, I have to go. Roger Anderson has burned himself on his new BBQ, and Myra's bringing him down to the clinic.' He avoided Jess's eyes, focussing on her chin.

Without waiting for a reply he ran up towards the Norfolk pines and the stairs leading to the main street and the clinic.

He ran for all he was worth, his gut churning, dread crawling across his skin. He could still feel those arms around him, pulling him in, sucking him down to a place he feared to go. A place that would only cause him pain.

He ran faster, welcoming the pain in his shins as his feet pounded on the concrete.

What had happened to maintaining an emotional distance? What had happened to avoiding children? When had the fun times merged with a sense of belonging? Everything had snuck up on him and exploded in his face.

And it scared him to death.

He reached the clinic before the Andersons, and leaned against the door, catching his breath. He closed his eyes, but the image of Jess and Woody filled the darkness.

He opened his eyes, fighting off the image. He wasn't part of their life. They were not part of his. He couldn't go down that road of love and family again. It cost too much.

He pushed open the door, the air-conditioned air chilling him. *I can't do this any more, David.* He reached for the phone and punched in some numbers. 'Get me the locum service for the south west district.'

It was time to go back to Melbourne.

Jess tucked Woody into bed with his much loved rabbit and kissed him goodnight. He was exhausted from his day in the fresh air, and happily snuggled down.

She tiptoed from his room and ran downstairs.

'All set?' Anna, sitting on the couch, looked up from her favourite TV show.

'He'll be asleep in about three minutes. Thanks for coming over on such short notice.' Jess squeezed the older woman's shoulder.

'No problem. Where are you off to?'

I have to talk to Alex. Jess hated lying to Anna, but explanations were all too hard. 'Friends of Elly and Patrick's are visiting, and they rang to ask if I could meet them for a drink.'

'That sounds fun. Have a great time.' Anna turned back to the TV.

Jess picked up her bag and headed out through the door into the night. A cool breeze blew off the bay, and she tugged her light jacket around her. The first stars shone in the dusky sky against the lingering pink of the sunset. She decided to walk down to Alex's house. The Parkinsons' house, the voice inside her head reminded her. Alex was just a temporary resident.

For the last couple of hours she'd been waiting for Alex's call. He usually rang after he'd been called away. He'd ring and tell her about the patient, and then say goodnight. And as they both knew Roger and Myra she was surprised he hadn't called to fill her in on Roger's burn.

Myra had rung Jess about something else, and had mentioned that Alex had dressed the burn in ten minutes and they'd been home again in time for a late dinner.

So it was odd he hadn't called. He'd looked very distracted at the beach just before his phone had rung. Perhaps Woody had kicked him in the ribs when he'd been clambering all over him.

She needed to see him. Needed to check he was all right. She wanted her goodnight.

Well, she'd get it in person. She'd call by and surprise him, say goodnight and enjoy a goodnight kiss for extra measure. She hugged her jacket close to her in anticipation.

They'd had so much fun on the beach. He'd been relaxed, and so wonderful with Woody. So natural. Balancing some boundaries with good old-fashioned family fun.

She could still feel the wondrous sensation of Woody and Alex pressed against her, hugging her in the sand.

He would have been a sensational father to Nick.

He'd be a wonderful father to Woody.

The thought struck her deep inside and her blood rushed to her feet. This time she'd fallen in love with a man who'd make a wonderful father. A kernel of hope sent up a tiny shoot. Had Alex joined them at the beach because he'd wanted to spend time with them both? Was this a first step forward with his life? Seeing relationships in a new light?

She did a little skip, the tiny kernel of hope inside her expanding.

No lights glowed from the front of the Parkinsons' house, but Alex's car was parked in the driveway. She walked along the side of the house around to the back deck, expecting to find him in the kitchen.

Swallowing a curse as she hit her ankle on the bottom veranda step, she was surprised to find the back half of the house in darkness as well.

Sliding the back door open, she stepped inside, flicked on the light and called out. 'Hello? Alex?'

The silence of the house contrasted starkly with the cacophony of the crickets' song.

Empty coffee mugs stood on side-tables, old newspapers lay scattered around the lounge room, and two packing boxes sat next to the couch.

Unease nibbled at her stomach. It would be a bit

hard to surprise him if she couldn't find him. She checked the rooms. All were empty.

She walked back out onto the deck. The noise of a group of young people partying on the beach drifted back to her. She stared out into the night.

The garden dropped away to the beach along a path lined with tea-tree, which cast black shadows. Grabbing David's large torch, which lived permanently on the deck, she started to walk down the path.

Anxiety skated along her veins. She was being ridiculous. Everything had a logical explanation. He was a doctor, for heaven's sake. He could be out on another emergency.

Acid shot into her stomach, churning and rumbling. She'd give herself an ulcer at this rate. She turned back to the deck. Flipping open her mobile phone, she checked for messages. None. She dialled his number. The call defaulted to the message bank. She didn't leave a message. She could dial his paging service, but that would show her to be too needy.

Well, she had the time—she would just wait. She sat down hard on the bottom step and focussed on the stars. Wishing on the stars.

'Jess, what are you doing here?' His voice came out of the darkness.

She jumped up, relief flooding her. 'I thought I'd surprise you.' She ran towards him, catching him in her arms.

'Well, you've done that.' He brushed her forehead with his lips in a distracted way.

A ripple of concern slithered through her. He'd never

kissed her with such disinterest before. 'It's a gorgeous night, so I thought a walk along the beach in the moonlight would be the perfect end to a fun day.' She rose on her tiptoes and kissed his mouth, her tongue flicking at his lips for entry.

For a brief moment he pressed against her and his lips started to part. Suddenly he pulled back. 'I don't fancy being eaten alive by mosquitoes. Let's go inside.'

Her stomach lurched as alarm shot through her. He always matched her passion. 'Where's your sense of adventure?'

'I'm going inside, Jess.'

The shadows of the night hid his expression, but his curt voice sent shivers chillingly down her spine.

Something had happened. In the last few hours, something terrible had happened. He'd shut down from her, distanced himself. Clenching her fists to her sides, she tried to steady the rising dread that lumped in her throat.

She let him walk ahead. Her legs didn't want to move. She didn't want to go inside and see his expression in the harsh artificial light. She didn't want to face him—face her fear of what he might say.

Gathering every ounce of strength she had, she willed herself to walk inside. She found him in the kitchen, the coffee pot in his hand. He didn't look at her.

Numbness filled her.

'Coffee?' He picked up a mug.

She sat down at the bench. 'That's a first.'

'Pardon?'

'You offering me coffee. You've offered me many things in this house, but never coffee.' She mustered a smile and touched his hand, hoping she'd imagined his coolness.

He withdrew his hand and sighed. 'Perhaps it's time I did.' He poured the cup and slid it across the bench. He remained standing, the kitchen bench between them.

Her heart twisted. 'I feel like I'm at a job interview.' The quip crashed into the thick silence.

Alex didn't speak. He stood staring into his coffee, his tension reaching out, cloaking her in suffocating heaviness.

Who was this man in front her? She didn't recognise him. Her loving Alex had vanished. Nothing about this man in front of her was familiar.

This was the man who had arrived in Roseport ten weeks ago.

Oh, God. The voice was right. The rigid tension, the strained expression, the distant aloofness and the shuttered eyes. All of it was back. In the wonder of the last few weeks she'd forgotten the Alex she'd first met.

Goosebumps generated by fear raised themselves like mountain ranges on her skin. Surely knowing the reason for his change in behaviour had to be better than not knowing.

'Alex, what's happened?'

He met her gaze, his normally sparkling eyes dull. 'I have to head back to Melbourne. I'm leaving tomorrow.'

Air rushed out of her lungs as his matter-of-fact voice pierced her heart. The walls of the room started to close in on her. He couldn't leave. Not yet.

'But David isn't back for two more weeks.' *Two weeks which belong to us.*

'I've arranged a locum who can start on Monday. I wouldn't leave Roseport without medical care.'

But you'd leave me. 'Well, that's good to know. Glad you're thinking about the town's wellbeing.' Sarcasm tripped off her tongue. She dragged in a breath. 'Why do you have to leave so suddenly?'

He shrugged his shoulders. 'All good things have to come to an end.'

She tried to ignore the hurtful jab. She knew his tactics, and he was deliberately stonewalling her. She pushed on. 'Why are you leaving two weeks early?'

He ploughed his hand through his hair. 'Jess, we said this would be a fun, temporary thing.'

Her stomach dropped. 'We did. But you've just changed the rules by cutting out early to rush back to a job you hate.'

He avoided looking at her. 'I do an important job in Melbourne.'

Frustration surged. 'Listen to yourself. You arrived in Roseport numbed by the interminable boringness of your job. You love the medicine here, yet you're running back to Melbourne early.'

'Don't be ridiculous,' he snapped back, too fast.

She'd hit a nerve. *Running away from me.* The thought struck her with the sting of a hard slap. But why was he running? Why today? She racked her brain. What had happened in the last few hours?

The image of the three of them on the beach pounded her. Woody on Alex's back, Alex's arms around her, his warm laughter and then his piercing, stricken look.

'You're running away from Woody and me.' She spoke the words flatly, the truth glaring and harsh. He couldn't stay. He was afraid to be part of their lives.

'I am not running away.' He spoke hastily.

He was. She knew it with every fibre of her being. She had to fight for him. He needed to realise what he was doing. 'Really? You've been running from Africa for two years, Alex. Nick wouldn't have wanted his wonderful father to scale his life back to a mere existence. He loved the vibrant man who showed him the world, taught him things and cherished him.'

This time the pain on his face didn't wound her. He needed to face the truth. She needed to speak it.

The words tumbled from her mouth unchecked. 'You've run from medicine by putting yourself into a dull, non-exacting job that won't ever force you to take a risk, won't ever let you lose a patient. You've shut down from people, hidden from relationships and hidden from children. I can understand why, but now it's time to stop just existing. It's time to start living and risk loving.' She reached out to touch him but he spun away.

'And you're an expert on living, are you?' He ground out the words.

'No, but at least I'm trying. You're scared to death because you enjoyed spending time with Woody. Now you're running away to hide. I'm not hiding from my life.'

'Aren't you? I think you're hiding behind Woody. You're so scared of falling in love again you put Woody up as your shield.'

His words hailed down on her, the truth denting her. 'Perhaps, but it didn't work. The shield was pierced a while ago.' The words echoed around the room, marking the air, unable to be taken back.

His face drained of colour and he ran his hands through his hair. 'Hell, Jess, you *can't* love me. Please don't love me.' His voice cracked.

Pain gripped her heart. 'It's too late. I already do.'

He shook his head in disbelief. 'We said it was temporary. We both went into this with our eyes open. Neither one of us wanted commitment. We didn't want a relationship. We said we'd walk away, no questions asked. That's why I'm leaving. I can't love you or Woody.' He drew in a ragged breath. 'I'm so sorry.'

His words, stark and bold, gave truth to what she already knew but had refused to acknowledge. His image wobbled in front of her tear-laden eyes. She bit her lip. Her head spun as the blood pounded loudly in her head.

He didn't love her.

Her chest ached. She had to leave; she had to get out of here with her dignity intact. Hauling the words out through a choked throat, she tried to keep the tremor out of her voice. 'Good luck with the rest of your life.'

She turned and wrenched open the door.

'Jess, I'll drive you home.' The softness and sympathy in his voice almost undid her.

'No!' The word shot out like a pellet from a gun. How dared he feel sorry for her? 'I don't need your help. Goodbye.' She ran outside and down to the beach, tears stinging her eyes, her heart bleeding in her chest.

It had happened again. She'd fallen in love with a man incapable of loving her back. A man blind to how wonderful his life could be with her and Woody. Only this time the pain was endless.

She sank down onto the damp sand, her anguished sobs buried against her pulled-up knees. Only fools thought they could control whom they fell in love with. She'd been living in a fool's paradise for the last ten weeks.

She dragged in a shuddering breath and looked out across the water, lit yellow by the full moon. Reality started *now*. Her life with Woody started *now*. She and Woody stood alone. Together they would forge ahead, creating their own small family. She had a little boy who loved her unconditionally.

It had to be enough.

CHAPTER TEN

JESS tugged rigorously at the weeds while perspiration trickled down her neck, dampening her T-shirt. Wiping her face on her sleeve, she sighed. She'd been working in the garden for most of the day, trying to keep busy. Trying not to think about Alex.

It wasn't working. The sharp pain inside her twisted and deepened. She glanced at her watch. Alex would have left town by now. She aimed weedkiller at the oxalis. Tomorrow morning she would front up to work and meet the locum. She squeezed the pump firmly and a fine spray coated the weed.

Woody's laugh roused her, and she turned to see him running through the sprinkler, squealing in delight. She wished her life could be as uncomplicated as a two-year-old's.

'I can't love you and Woody.' Alex's words beat a tattoo in her brain, each beat hurting more.

The sun beat down on her. She was sick of weeding and tired of thinking. Hot and filled with heartache, she needed to do something to drive Alex's words out of her head.

Kicking off her shoes, she stood up. 'Coming to get you!' She sprinted through the sprinkler towards Woody, gasping as the cold water soaked her.

She dodged and wove around the sprinkler, chasing him, her shrieks and laughter matching his childish pleasure. She caught him and swung him high in an arc through the water.

Focussing on Woody would get her through her heartache.

Short of breath, she collapsed onto the grass to rest. Woody crawled into her lap, his wet body resting against her. 'Biccy, please?' Hope reflected in his eyes.

Jess laughed. 'Why not? It's afternoon teatime.' She wrapped him in a towel and dropped a kiss onto his wet curls. 'Sit here and I'll get you a drink and a biscuit.'

She ran inside and quickly poured an apple juice, and grabbed a lemon soda for herself. Opening the biscuit barrel, she munched on an Anzac and put two others on a plastic plate.

Balancing the plate on top of the drink can, she held Woody's cup in the other hand and pushed the flywire door open with her bottom. Woody had wandered over to the woodpile.

'Woody, I've got your biscuits.'

Woody swung around quickly, dropping the bucket he was holding, and took one step towards her. Suddenly he screamed and crumpled to the ground.

Jess's heart lodged in her throat and the drinks and biscuits tumbled from her hands. She sprinted to him. As she reached him she saw the brown tail of a snake slithering back into the woodpile.

Panic surged in her chest. Reaching down, she hauled Woody into her arms and moved him away.

'Leg hurt.' Woody sobbed hysterically, clutching his calf.

'Show me.' She ran her hands down his leg, pulling his hands away. Fang marks punctured the pale skin of his leg.

Snake bite.

Snake bite.

Shafts of fear sliced through her, searing her with pain. Immobilising her. She struggled to breathe. She struggled to think against the black fear roaring in her head.

The snake's tail—what had it looked like? She tried to push through the fog of fear and think. *Brown.* Brown. It could be a copperhead or an Eastern Brown. Both had venom which could kill a child quickly.

She clutched him to her, holding him tight.

Oh, God, she'd only had Woody for a short time, and now he could be snatched away from her. Like everyone she loved.

No!

A surge of adrenaline swooped through her, bringing the nurse into control. Hauling herself to her feet, she cradled Woody close and ran towards the house.

Woody clung to her, his warm tears soaking into her cold, wet shirt as she stumbled through the wire door. Grabbing the cordless phone, she punched in 000 with shaking fingers. The operator promised her an ambulance from Ryeton.

'Sweetheart, I need to make you feel better. You need to lie on the couch.' She tried to lie Woody down, but he screamed and clung to her.

Woody pulled his legs up and cried. 'Tummy hurts.'

Nausea, vomiting and abdominal pain are common with snake bite. Keep the victim still. Don't clean the wound as it interferes with venom identification.

First aid screamed in her head, making her dizzy. She needed to stay calm.

Immobilise the bitten leg.

Bandages.

She didn't dare put Woody down; he had to stay as still as possible. Somehow, with Woody clinging to her, she managed to climb onto a chair up to the first-aid kit stored high in the kitchen cupboard, away from inquisitive little boys.

Grabbing the crêpe bandages, she climbed down and headed back to the couch. 'Sweetie, I have to put a special bandage on your leg to make it feel better.'

Bandage above and below the puncture site, immobilising the limb.

She cradled Woody on her lap and with shaking hands wound the bandage around his small leg from toes to groin. Firm, but not so tight as to cut off his circulation. The bandage should slow the spread of the venom to the rest of his body.

She prayed it would work. It *had* to work. She couldn't lose him.

Hugging him close, with his heart hammering against her chest, she wanted to stroke him and kiss away his fear.

It was a luxury she didn't have. The nurse in her drove her on.

Antivenom. Woody needed it.

Think.

The clinic had antivenom. How could she get it? The clinic was closed. Still holding Woody tightly on her lap, keeping him still, she rang the emergency number, hoping it would default to the new locum or Anna. *Someone.*

Anna answered the phone.

'It's Jess. I need antivenom. Woody's been bitten by a snake but I don't know what type.'

'Oh, God, no.' Anna's shock permeated down the line.

Jess forced herself to speak slowly and clearly. 'The antivenom is in the clinic fridge. Please bring it over with the emergency medical kit.'

'I'm on my way.' The line went dead.

She stroked Woody's head, sang 'Baa Baa Black Sheep' to help calm him, and strained her ears for the ambulance siren.

'Bunny, Bunny.' Woody cried for his favourite soft toy.

Jess whirled around, her gaze searching wildly for his rabbit. Spying it under a chair, she snatched it up. 'Here he is, and he needs a big cuddle.'

She ran her hand over Woody's forehead. Beads of sweat wet her palm.

Woody pulled his legs up towards his chin and vomited.

The black cavern of fear inside her deepened. Pushing her hand against her mouth, she stifled a scream. The venom was taking hold. What if the poison paralysed his heart and lungs before he got to hospital?

Woody closed his eyes.

Terror lanced her. She nudged him, and his eyes fluttered open for a second before quickly closing again. She dropped to her knees and stroked his head. Where the hell was help?

* * *

Alex swore silently at the pile of S2 forms on his desk. The Parkinsons' house was clean, and the car was packed, but he couldn't leave for Melbourne until the dreaded paperwork was complete.

Pulling out his fountain pen, he sat down. Once he'd finished the S2s he was leaving Roseport for good. He stared at the neat stack. A bright-coloured Post-it note stuck to the first form, covered in Jess's neat script.

Well done on getting started. There's a surprise at the finish.

She'd put a smiley face next to the word 'finish'.

An image of her leaning against the office door, arms folded across her chest, giving him her best impersonation of a schoolmarm while her eyes twinkled, filled him. She'd always teased him about his avoidance of paperwork. She'd teased him about a lot of things, and it had filled him with a lightness he now missed.

The ache inside him deepened.

He turned on the CD player, cranking up the volume, using the music to drive away her image. He'd made his choice. He couldn't stay in Roseport. He couldn't give her what she wanted. He couldn't love her or Woody. Wouldn't allow himself to even think he could.

Love meant loss and grief, and to survive he couldn't love again. Leaving Roseport was the right decision. The best decision for everyone.

He pulled the next form towards him. Two down, forty-eight to go.

A pounding on the door startled him. He walked briskly down the corridor and pulled open the door.

Anna stood clutching the clinic keys, her hands shaking and her face white. 'I saw your car. Thank God you're here. A snake has bitten Jess's nephew and she needs antivenom.'

Woody.

Jess.

Bile scalded his throat. He clenched his fists, willing himself to stay calm, fighting the cloud of fear that threatened to descend. He turned towards the treatment room. 'What sort of snake?'

'She isn't sure. It could be an Eastern Brown, a Copperhead or a Tiger Snake, all of them live around here. Whichever it was, it isn't good.' Anna spoke quickly as she followed him down the corridor.

He raced into the treatment room and hauled the fridge open. Where the hell was the polyvalent antivenom? Vials and ampoules neatly lined up in trays stared back at him.

He frantically scanned them all, the words blurring in his haste. He dragged in a calming breath. He couldn't let fear paralyse him. He was no use to Woody or Jess if he couldn't think.

He located the rubber-topped vial of polyvalent antivenom and placed it in a cooler pack. Picking up the pack and his medical bag, he ran past Anna. 'I'll ring you.'

Gunning the car, he drove the short distance to Shore Crest Road. His heart pounded. Jess would be frantic with worry and fear. Nothing could ever prepare you for the deluge of emotions that swamped you when your child lay threatened. He knew that feeling too well.

He didn't want Jess to have to experience it.

Woody couldn't die.

He ran around the back of the house, wrenched open the door and rushed in.

Jess knelt beside the couch, her back to him. He wanted to run to her, hold her, tell her everything would be all right. But he couldn't promise what he didn't know—what he might not be able to deliver.

She moved and he caught sight of Woody, motionless on the couch.

An image of Nick, deathly white on a stretcher, blasted into him. Every muscle in his body froze.

Every moment of the last few hours of Nick's life flashed through his brain like a DVD on fast-forward. He'd done all he could for Nick and it hadn't been enough.

A spasm of dread jerked through him. What if he couldn't do enough for Woody?

He breathed deeply, and a shaft of clarity pierced the dread. He couldn't think like that. He was a doctor, and he'd do everything in his power to save Jess's little boy.

'Jess.'

She turned at the sound of his voice. Anguish and shock lined her beautiful face, followed quickly by confusion.

He didn't blame her. He was the last person she would have expected to see. Probably the last person she wanted to see. *I can't love you.* The words that had caused her so much pain boomed in his head.

She scrambled to her feet, and he saw the control enter her body. 'Thank you for coming.' She spoke as if greeting a vague acquaintance. 'He needs a doctor.

He needs a doctor.

That was how she saw him, purely as a doctor. Not a friend, just a doctor. Damn, what had he expected after the way he'd treated her? He didn't know, but he hated the coolness in her tone.

'I've bandaged his leg, but he's floating in and out of consciousness. He needs antivenom.' Expectation lined her face. She believed he would save her child.

Terror of failing tore at him.

Jess couldn't lose Woody. Jess shouldn't have to go through what he'd been through. He had to save him.

Dragging on every resource he had, he swung into doctor mode, visualising Woody as a patient, not a kid who'd touched his heart. Visualising Jess as a mother, not his ex-lover.

He was the doctor.

'I've brought the polyvalent antivenom.' He dumped his bag on the table and snapped open the latches.

'I'm not certain what type of snake it was.' Her voice trembled. 'It happened so quickly.'

'Well, the polyvalent is the one to use, then. Once he's at Ryeton we can use the venom identification kit and determine exactly what type of snake it was, then use a specific antivenom.'

'But Ryeton doesn't have a paediatric ICU.' Her words came out in a terrified wail.

He touched her arm briefly, trying to calm her. She stiffened at the contact and he removed his hand. 'If he needs to be transferred we'll deal with that. Right now, let's administer the antivenom.' He pulled an IV cannula and flow-set from his bag. 'It needs to be administered through Hartmann's Solution.'

'Will he react to it?' The tremor in her voice pulled at him.

'He might, because it contains animal serum, so we'll have adrenaline on stand-by.'

'I'll draw it up.' She reached into the medical kit.

He touched her arm again and fixed her with his gaze. 'It's OK, Jess, you stay with Woody.'

'I've got to do something.' Her hands balled at her sides. 'I feel so helpless.'

He knew that feeling. 'I understand, but we're doing everything we can.'

'It mightn't be enough.' Her bald words reflected his dread.

'It has to be.' He wrapped the tourniquet around Woody's tiny arm and gently probed for a vein.

Nothing.

Venous shutdown. He swallowed the expletive he wanted to shout.

Jess's gaze, full of naked fear, followed his fingers. 'Alex, you have to find a vein. Do a venous cutdown if you need to.'

He wrenched his gaze from hers. He couldn't bear to see her pain. He wanted to hold her, hug her to him, stroke her hair and banish her fear.

But he had to save her child first.

He moved the tourniquet to Woody's foot on the unbandaged leg. He breathed out a silent prayer of thanks. A slight bulge pulsed under his finger. 'Hold Jess's hand, mate. This might hurt.'

Woody barely responded.

He swabbed the area, the alcohol scent stinging his

nostrils. Sliding the needle gently under the skin, he guided it into the vein. Blood flowed back. 'Connect the Hartmann's.'

Jess pushed the IV into the cannula while he taped it in place.

She nudged him aside. 'I'll do that. Give him the antivenom. He could be starting to clot.' Her words struck with staccato firmness.

He recognised her behaviour. Two years ago he'd been the same. Trying to get control over a situation where he'd had none. 'He needs forty thousand units.' He punctured the rubber bung on the vial with the large bore needle and withdrew the antivenom. Quickly transferring the antivenom into the burette, he diluted it with the Hartmann's Solution. 'I'll titrate it in over an hour.'

'Will it work in time? Will it stop him clotting? Will he need intubation?' The strain on Jess's face had etched deep lines around her eyes and mouth. She knew too much, and all her knowledge terrified her.

'I can't tell you that. We have to hope it will.' God, he sounded like a doctor—but being a doctor was the only thing getting them through this. She wanted reassurance. He couldn't give it.

He checked Woody's pulse. Thready.

Come on, mate. Fight. Stay with us. Hang in there.

The scream of the ambulance centred him.

Mick ran in. 'Geez, Jess, I'm so sorry.' He enveloped her in a brief hug.

Alex swore under his breath. Mick had given Jess the comfort she needed and she'd accepted it. He'd tried and she'd flinched at his touch.

You're only the doctor.

To hell with that. He moved forward to the couch and gathered Woody into his arms, ignoring the surprised look on Mick's face. 'Come on, Mick. Carry the IV.'

He strode out towards the rig, feeling Woody's heart pounding against his own chest.

''Lex…' Woody's eyes fluttered open for a moment.

The trust in Woody's eyes hit him in the solar plexus. 'It's OK, mate, I'm right here—and so is Jess.' He gently laid him down onto the stretcher and attached an oxygen mask. The cardiac monitor dots stood out starkly against Woody's white skin, making him look like fragile porcelain.

Fight, little boy. Stay with us.

Jess clambered into the back of the ambulance, hauling herself up.

Instinctively, he shot his hand out to help her in, expecting her to reject his help.

But her hand gripped his and he pulled her into his arms. 'Jess, we're going to fight this venom with everything medical science has got.'

She nodded mutely, tears glistening in her eyes, and for a brief moment she buried her head in his shoulder.

He held her, stroking her back, trying to soothe and comfort, needing to have her in his arms.

Abruptly she moved away and positioned herself next to Woody, stroking his hair and holding his hand. 'I love you, sweetie.'

She'd shut him out. Woody was hers alone, not his to share. Mother and child as a solid unit, existing together, surviving alone.

Wasn't that what he'd wanted? Not to be involved? His arms ached with emptiness. Now he had what he wanted.

Suddenly it felt very wrong.

Five hours later, exhaustion seeped out of his every pore. Alex took a long draught of hospital coffee and re-read Woody's blood results, tuning out the constant beeping and huffing noise of Intensive Care.

He put down the results and walked over to Woody, who lay sedated and intubated, his blaze of red hair the only colour in the clinical environment. Surrounded by monitors and pumps, and with a central line and a urinary catheter inserted into his small body, it was hard to make out the special little boy from the equipment.

Alex checked Woody's vital signs again. His blood pressure was erratic and his urine output borderline, but at least his fibrinogen levels had come into normal range. The risk of clotting had lessened. The specific antivenom for the Eastern Brown snake now dripped into his small body, mopping up the venom, giving Woody's body a fighting chance.

The frantic pace of the last few hours had finally slowed. He'd done everything he could for Woody. Now they waited.

As much as he hated that Woody was desperately ill, he couldn't ignore the buzz he'd got from working in ICU. Jess was right. His Melbourne job was boring. David had been right too, about Roseport helping him find his love of medicine again. As soon as Woody was off the critical list he'd be looking for a new job in Melbourne. A job with hands-on medicine.

He stroked the lock of hair that had fallen across the little boy's forehead. Woody's childish voice sounded in his head. *Play Scuffy, 'Lex. Build castle.* The sensation of chubby hands tugging at his legs, of the warm, cuddly child in his lap, tore through him.

What if he never held Woody again?

Fear jetted up inside him like a geyser and a chill settled over him, the coldness seeping into his veins. 'Hey, little man.' He spoke softly. 'You won't remember today's ride in a helicopter, but I'll take you on one when you're better.' Hell, he was bargaining. He ran his hands through his hair. 'Come on, Woody, you have to fight.'

Fight for me.

The words bellowed in his head. Loud and constant. Suddenly he knew. Suddenly, with crystal-clear clarity, he knew he wanted to feel Woody's chubby hands in his own again, wanted to cuddle him in his lap, wanted to see him grow, teach him how to fly a kite, build a treehouse and hug him close.

He loved this little boy.

Woody was as dear to him as Nick. Losing him would hurt just as much.

The knowledge stunned him. He'd been so busy protecting his heart, yet Woody had managed to sneak in under his armour. He'd tried not to love, but it had happened anyway.

He glanced over at Jess, who slept in a chair. Exhaustion had finally claimed her. She looked fragile but her inner strength amazed him.

She'd forced him to examine his life. Her words surrounded him. *Nick wouldn't have wanted his wonderful father to scale his life back to mere existence.*

She was right; he'd gone into a holding pattern, had been existing not living, and he'd been fighting off anyone who tried to get close to him.

Including Jess. His beautiful Jess.

Damn it, yesterday he'd acted like a fool, distancing himself from the two most precious people in his life.

He loved her.

The thought slammed into him so hard he gripped the IV pole.

How had he been so blind to what he'd had? Was it too late to reverse the damage? It better not be. It was time to stop running.

It was time to start loving.

Jess's shoulders ached, and a hot white pain shot through her neck when she moved. Sleep fled and she opened her eyes, hoping it had all been a nightmare.

It wasn't. She was in a chair in Intensive Care at the Royal Children's Hospital in Melbourne.

She reached out and touched her darling little boy and bit her lip. Holding his hand, stroking his hair, washing him—that was all she could do for him. It wasn't anywhere near enough.

Woody's respirator whooshed in and out, its rhythm engraved on her memory. She strained to listen for any irregularities, a sign that Woody's lungs were working independently. But the respirator was regular—twelve breaths per minute—the machine was doing all the work.

Alex stood on the other side of the bed, checking

Woody's central venous pressure. A fine stubble of blond hair covered his jaw and lines of fatigue ringed his eyes, the signs of a battle-weary soldier.

He'd kept a constant vigil, worry etched into his face like charcoal on white paper. Even when they'd arrived at the Royal Children's he'd stayed actively involved in Woody's treatment.

She'd tried to stay aloof from him. She wished she'd had the strength to insist he didn't need to be here, that Woody wasn't his to worry about. But having him in the same room made this nightmare easier to bear.

She noticed the tender way he touched Woody and the tear in her heart ripped a little more. He couldn't see that he loved Woody, that he'd make a wonderful father and by leaving he was turning his back on happiness.

'Jess.' He spoke her name softly. 'Take a break.'

'I'm fine.'

'No, you're not. You need a break, and some food.' Concern filled his eyes, more green than ever against the hospital scrubs.

She fought the urge to throw herself into his arms and take refuge there, breathing in his strength. 'I'm not leaving him.'

'You won't be leaving him. I'm here.'

For now, but you'll leave us. She shook her head. 'I'm staying.'

'I'll organise some sandwiches for you.' He caught the eye of one of the nurses who had been with them for the last six hours.

'Not a problem, Dr Fitzwilliam.' The young woman

flashed a smile as she walked off, hips swaying, to telephone the kitchen.

A flash of jealousy ripped through Jess and she bit her tongue to prevent herself speaking her thoughts. *You're wasting your time; he can't love anyone any more.*

She stood up and fiddled with Woody's top sheet even though it lay neat and flat. She needed to do something, and yelling and screaming weren't allowed. So she fidgeted instead.

Concentrating on breathing deeply to stay calm, she listened to the respirator, letting its regular sounds soothe her.

Suddenly the respirator hiccoughed.

Had she heard right? 'Alex?' She forced his name through her constricted throat.

He turned towards her, his face alive with a smile. A smile she hadn't seen since she'd lain in his arms at the beach.

Her heart beat erratically. 'Did you hear that?'

He nodded excitedly. 'He's triggering the respirator. He's trying to breathe on his own. If he can keep that up we'll be able to extubate him pretty soon.'

He moved to her side. 'You know what that means?' He wrapped his arm around her shoulder, gathering her close. 'He's going to be all right. He's going to run on the beach and play with Scuffy and dig in the sand.'

Joy surged through her. Tears and laughter collided in her throat and she gave in to the need to touch him, burying her face in his shoulder. His heat and energy flooded her. 'Oh, thank God.'

For the briefest of moments everything felt right.

Then reality intruded. Now Woody had turned the corner Alex would leave, and take her heart with him. With her last ounce of energy she broke contact and stepped back, raising her eyes to his. 'Thanks for staying—for being his doctor.' She bit her lip and kept going. She refused to break down. 'It meant a lot to both of us.'

Shock marked his face and he paled. 'You thought I might leave?' His voice came out in a horrified whisper. 'Of course I was going to stay with him. I couldn't have left you or our little boy in the company of strangers.'

Our little boy.

The three words bounced in her brain like an erratic squash ball. She closed her eyes, trying desperately to catch the thought and make sense of it.

Her legs started to shake. Did he realise what he'd just said?

'Our little boy?'

He nodded and reached for her hand. 'Jess, I've been a fool. You were right. I've been running. When Nick died part of me died with him.' His thumb caressed her hand in circles. 'I never wanted to love anyone that much again. I had the crazy thought that if I didn't love I could never lose. Then I met you.'

Her heart hammered hard and fast against her ribs. 'I…' Words jammed in her throat.

He gently cupped her chin with one hand and stroked her lips with his thumb. 'Please, I need to explain. You deserve to hear this. I cringe when I think of what I said to you last night, and if I could turn back time I would. I'm so very sorry that I hurt you.'

Her heart dared to hope, and she forced her stunned mind to focus on his words.

His arm circled her waist, but he didn't draw her any closer. 'You've given me colour in my grey life. When I'm in your arms I have an overwhelming sense of peace. The peace I've been looking for since Nick died. But I've been slow to see it, and I've spent too much time fighting it.'

His sincerity tore at her. 'It scared you?'

He nodded. 'You know me too well. It scared the hell out of me. But tonight, when I thought we might lose Woody, I realised I have to love to live—and life without the two of you in it isn't living.' He pulled her in hard against him. 'I love you, Jess, with all my heart. And I love Woody. The three of us belong together.'

She let his words wrap around her heart, sealing him to her. Reaching out her hand, she stroked his cheek. 'I think I've loved you from the moment I met you, looking so out of place in an Armani suit in a beach resort.' Her voice cracked. 'And I love the way you love our little boy.'

His eyes scanned her face. 'Will you stay with me for ever? Long after Woody and his brothers and sisters have left home?'

A family—their family. Her heart almost burst with happiness. 'I'll treasure every minute.'

His emerald eyes, scored deeply with love, scanned her face. 'Marry me?'

Tears filled her eyes and she nodded furiously. 'I will. I most certainly will.'

He ducked his head, capturing her lips in a kiss of

love, passion and permanence. His energy mixed with hers, making her part of him and binding them together for ever.

EPILOGUE

ALEX'S hands rested over Woody's as the stunt kite soared overhead. 'Let's make it loop the loop.'

Woody's left hand pulled down by his side and the kite dived and then soared again high above Roseport. He looked up into a pair of green eyes alive with excitement. 'That's so cool, Dad.'

Not that Alex was his real dad, but he was the only dad he'd ever known. He liked to think that Dad's son Nick and his own real dad spent time together in heaven, flying kites. He made sure their pictures were always next to each other on the mantelpiece. It made him feel better about things. About the fact he got to do so much cool stuff with Alex.

'Hey, you two, that looks like fun. Can I have a go?'

Woody groaned. If Mum wanted to fly the kite that meant he had to play the Scuffy game with the twins. They just loved pulling the tugboat through the water and filling it with periwinkles. Maybe he could convince them to help him build a huge sand fort.

He ran back towards the twins. Lucy was chasing

seagulls, and Fletcher was trying to bury the plastic boatmen.

'Come on, Fletch, let's build a castle.' Being the big brother of three-year-old twins was a responsibility. 'We'll show Mum and Dad what we can do.'

Ten minutes later he sat back and surveyed their handiwork. He looked over towards his adopted parents. Mum was leaning back into Dad, their heads close together. The kite flew wonkily around the sky.

Cuddling again. Man, they were always cuddling, and kissing and laughing.

The kite plunged into the sand. He ran over to them, the twins following. 'Mum, you need to keep your arms straight.' He shook his head in despair.

Her brown eyes twinkled. 'Sorry, Woody. I'll concentrate better next time.'

She pulled him towards her and gave him a hug. Thank goodness none of his friends were on the beach. He hugged her back.

The twins threw themselves at him, and Mum overbalanced against Dad. All of them landed in a heap on the sand, a tangle of arms and legs and shrieks of laughter.

'Did I ever tell you that I love you all so much?' Dad's deep voice wrapped around him.

Woody rolled his eyes. 'Every day, Dad.'

'And that Roseport is the best place in the world?'

'Yes, Dad.'

'Good. Then all's right in the Fitzwilliam family.'

And Woody had to agree with that.

First comes love, then comes marriage...

SUSAN MALLERY
FALLING FOR GRACIE

That was Gracie's plan, anyway, at the ripe old age of fourteen. She loved eighteen-year-old heart throb Riley with a legendary desperation. Even now that she's all grown up, the locals in her sleepy town won't let her forget her youthful crush.

...but it's not as easy as it looks.
And now she's face-to-face with Riley at every turn. The one-time bad boy has come back seeking respectability – but the sparks that fly between them are anything but respectable! Gracie's determined to keep her distance, but when someone sets out to ruin both their reputations, the two discover that first love sometimes is better the second time around.

On sale 1st September 2006

www.millsandboon.co.uk

M&B

MILLS & BOON®
Live the emotion

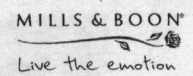

Medical
romance™

RESCUE AT CRADLE LAKE by Marion Lennox

Top surgeon Fergus hopes to soothe his broken heart with life at Cradle Lake – something which just might be possible with the help of local emergency doctor Ginny Viental. Is Fergus ready to make a life with Ginny, and her little niece? Especially when it means taking on a role he thought he would never face again – that of a father.

A NIGHT TO REMEMBER by Jennifer Taylor

A&E DRAMA

A tanker loaded with toxic chemicals is headed straight for an oil rig. A team, led by Dr Seb Bridges, is ready and waiting. Meanwhile, Dr Libby Bridges is on her way to ask Seb for a divorce... For Seb only two things matter: saving lives and saving his marriage. This will be the most important night of his life. And the clock is ticking...

A SURGEON, A MIDWIFE: A FAMILY
by Gill Sanderson

Dell Owen Maternity

Neonatal surgeon Jack Sinclair has learned to keep his professional and personal life separate. Until Dell Owen Hospital's new midwife, Miranda Gale, joins the team and breaks through his cool, detached façade. While Miranda is just as attracted to Jack, she has a secret...

On sale 6th October 2006

Available at WHSmith, Tesco, ASDA, Borders, Eason, Sainsbury's and most bookshops

www.millsandboon.co.uk

MILLS & BOON

Live the emotion

Medical romance™

THE DOCTOR'S NEW-FOUND FAMILY
by Laura MacDonald

Renowned surgeon Nathan Carrington has put his marriage behind him, and devoted his attention to his young son. Paediatrician Olivia Gilbert's world has been turned upside down – now she lives for her children. But Nathan and Olivia discover that single parenthood just isn't enough…

HER VERY SPECIAL CONSULTANT
by Joanna Neil

Dr Amelie Clarke's first day at work doesn't go as expected when she is rushed into A & E – as a patient. She is mortified that her gorgeous new boss, Gage Bracken, has seen her in her underwear! But caring for her four-year-old nephew combined with her job leaves Amelie no time for romance. Having healed her body, it is up to Gage to heal her heart as well.

THE ITALIAN DOCTOR'S BRIDE
by Margaret McDonagh

Mediterranean Doctors

Dr Nic di Angelis's arrival has stirred considerable interest in the rural Scottish village of Lochanrig! The GP has won the hearts of the whole community – apart from that of his boss, Dr Hannah Frost. It will take all of Nic's powers to break through Hannah's defences. Only then can Hannah fully embrace all that the fiery Italian has to offer…

On sale 6th October 2006

Available at WHSmith, Tesco, ASDA, Borders, Eason, Sainsbury's and most bookshops

www.millsandboon.co.uk

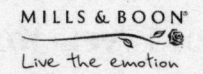

From No. 1 *New York Times* bestselling author Nora Roberts

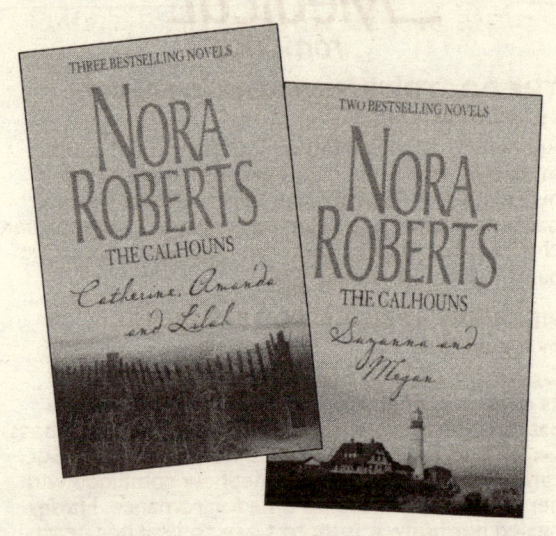

Atop the rocky coast of Maine sits the Towers, a magnificent family mansion that is home to a legend of long-lost love, hidden emeralds— and four determined sisters.

Catherine, Amanda & Lilah
available 4th August 2006

Suzanna & Megan
available 6th October 2006

Available at WHSmith, Tesco, ASDA, Borders, Eason, Sainsbury's and all good paperback bookshops

www.silhouette.co.uk

Can you tell from first impressions whether someone could become your closest friend?

Lydia, Jacqueline, Carol and Alix are four very different women, each facing their own problems in life. When they are thrown together by the hands of fate, none of them could ever guess how close they would become or where their friendship would lead them.

A heartfelt, emotional tale of friendship and problems shared from a multi-million copy bestselling author.

On sale 18th August 2006

FREE!

4 Books
and a surprise gift!

We would like to take this opportunity to thank you for reading this Mills & Boon® book by offering you the chance to take FOUR more specially selected titles from the Medical Romance™ series absolutely FREE! We're also making this offer to introduce you to the benefits of the Mills & Boon® Reader Service™—

- ★ FREE home delivery
- ★ FREE gifts and competitions
- ★ FREE monthly Newsletter
- ★ Exclusive Reader Service offers
- ★ Books available before they're in the shops

Accepting these FREE books and gift places you under no obligation to buy, you may cancel at any time, even after receiving your free shipment. Simply complete your details below and return the entire page to the address below. You don't even need a stamp!

YES! Please send me 4 free Medical Romance books and a surprise gift. I understand that unless you hear from me, I will receive 6 superb new titles every month for just £2.80 each, postage and packing free. I am under no obligation to purchase any books and may cancel my subscription at any time. The free books and gift will be mine to keep in any case.

M6ZEF

Ms/Mrs/Miss/Mr .... Initials ....
BLOCK CAPITALS PLEASE
Surname ....
Address ....
....
.... Postcode ....

Send this whole page to:
UK: FREEPOST CN81, Croydon, CR9 3WZ

Offer valid in UK only and is not available to current Mills & Boon® Reader Service™ subscribers to this series. Overseas and Eire please write for details. We reserve the right to refuse an application and applicants must be aged 18 years or over. Only one application per household. Terms and prices subject to change without notice. Offer expires 31st December 2006. As a result of this application, you may receive offers from Harlequin Mills & Boon and other carefully selected companies. If you would prefer not to share in this opportunity please write to The Data Manager, PO Box 676, Richmond, TW9 1WU.

Mills & Boon® is a registered trademark owned by Harlequin Mills & Boon Limited.
Medical Romance™ is being used as a trademark. The Mills & Boon® Reader Service™ is being used as a trademark.